Broken Sanity

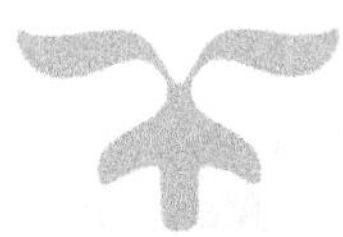

MICHAEL PERRY ALLEN

2025

LCCN #

ISBN # 979-8-9993765-2-7

TABLE OF CONTENTS

LARRY MEETS MARGARET 1

DATING A BOMBER PILOT 15

SITTING IN THE DARK 25

TWO OF A KIND 35

TAMPERED EVIDENCE 45

A DELICATE CONVERSATION 59

DEPLOYMENT 73

THE SECRET PORCH SOCIETY 85

INSTINCTS PREVAIL 99

WEDDING DAY 110

THE WIRE 119

A JOURNAL ENTRY 131

LAST NIGHT 141

THREE RINGS 151

THE A.T.M. VIDEO 161

NOT ADMISSIBLE 171

POOL SIDE 183

THE MEETING 195

TURN OF EVENTS 209

LOUISIANNA 221

CLOSING IN ON THE TRUTH 231

CASE CLOSED 245

Larry Meets Margaret

Leonard B. Rawlings (Lenny) was born January 11, 1975, in Bozier city, Louisianna.

The prominent son of Margaret and Larry Rawlings.

Lenny's father, a graduate of Louisianna State University where he studied aeronautic aviation. Utilizing a government funded program aptly named the (G.I. bill) helped Larry achieve an education that his parents were unable to provide.

After graduation it was necessary to fulfill the required obligation for accessing these funds and enlist in the U.S. Airforce at Barksdale Air Force Base. With his education and limited experience in flying anything other than a kite in an open field, Larry was quickly promoted to the status of captain.

After initial basic cadet training and the Airforce flying academy, Larry received orders to relocate to Mac-Dill Air Force Base in Tampa, Florida. Arriving in Tampa Larry began settling into the area while getting acclimated to the Florida sunshine.

Larry was a medium build man sporting the typical mandatory military style flat top haircut. A service requirement dating back several years when lice was prevalent in men's hair. Thus, generating the rules for short haircuts was the ideal way to control the spread and prevent further escalation of the annoying bugs to other soldiers.

Larry was man with a significantly higher intellect than the normal individual. Anyone encountering him-quickly acknowledges this and became his friend. One set of new friends introduced him to the game of golf along with the hot sandy beaches where he began spending most of his weekends relaxing on an old wooden beach chair set close enough to the water's edge where he could feel the waves crest across his feet.

One weekend while sitting at the Oceanfront outdoor hotspot called the "Sandbar" in the Opal Sands Resort. He was enjoying the scenery with the company of other Air Force pilots from the airbase. The first round of drinks was now served with the food order placed with a wait staff that Larry found strikingly attractive in every detail, constantly watching her attending to other customers throughout the restaurant.

So intrigued by this new mysterious woman, Larry commanded the attention of his fellow aviators and polled the accompanying group to see if they knew anything about the experienced staff member serving them that day.

No one had a clue who she was as one boisterous aviator with a playful inebriated voice announced he would volunteer his services to ask the young lady if she would not mind coming back to the table to introduce herself so they could all get to know her on a first name basis.

With all agreeing to the gesture, a toast was raised to confirm the one who suggested the idea should be the man to address the situation and report back to the group. At the end of the first toast another toast was raised as another member expressed great speed to his journey and a healthy return should he get slapped in the face in the process.

All beverages were once again raised as the man of the hour gulped his remaining liquid refreshment and proceeded to stumble away from the table. Although unknown to Larry at the time, his fellow soldier had an alternative plan up his sleeve as they diligently watched their hero approach the beautiful staff member.

Larry's eyes were now fixated on the two engaging in a moment of conversation. The timeline slowed; this scene was playing out like a slow-motion movie. To no one's surprise, they all witnessed a beautifully brilliant smile beginning to form on her face revealing a full set of white teeth, lighting up the room, every airman corrected his posture, fiddled with their hair, returning the same wide open smile back towards her, then observed, this beautiful; turned to look directly at Larry as she extended her arm toward their table, pointing her finger at the group.

Now returning her head to continue her conversation, nodding in acceptance. Departing from her concierge, she took another quick glance at the group of intoxicated sweaty young men sporting their military style butch haircuts and puffing out their chests, like a gorilla in a cage.

Returning to the table, the chosen crew member took his seat, without uttering a word, reached for his beer and began sipping his drink as if nothing had happened. The entire table fell silent. With all eyes trained on their hero, he said nothing.

Larry became anxious for a report, leaned forward from his chair, looked directly at his silent friend, with one word from his lips, breaking the deadlocked silence, he sternly asked.

"WELL?"

Stopping the bottle of beer that had just reached his friends' lips, the team and Larry received the reply they had been waiting for.

"I did not get her name, but she did say, she would be over her as soon as our food is ready. So, be patient."

Broken Sanity

No sooner than he spoke his words. The pilot quickly raised his hand while pointing his own finger in the direction of the bar, to report.

"Oh! look here she comes."

All heads turned as their eyes were now trained on the new wait staff approaching their table, holding a large tray filled with burgers and tacos, she reached her destination. With a smooth motion she turned away from the group to bend over at the waist setting the large tray on a folding stand next to their table.

Every man at the table leaned forward, using two fingers to pull down their aviator style sunglasses as all eyes were now focused on her backside.

She began placing everyone's order on the table in front of the respective person, except Larry. She stopped for a moment, holding the last order in her right hand, and turned to face Larry, engaging in direct eye contact as she begins to speak directly to him.

"So, I have been informed by your friend you are a bomber pilot interested in asking me out on a date. Is this true or not? If this is true I will give you your food. If it is not, your prankster friend will be paying for your lunch because he will be wearing it shortly. So, what is your answer to that Mr. Air Force Bomber pilot?"

Larry was shocked into silence, while everyone else seated at the table erupted in laughter. They were already informed of what was to come from the pre-planned approach of the wait staff. When Larry failed to answer her right away, another question shook him out of the trance he was in.

Broken Sanity

"Are you going to answer me or what? LARRY! By the way my first name is Margaret, you can get my family name after you answer me."

Larry finally found the courage to reply as he stood up to face Margaret like a gentleman, he replied.

"Great to meet you Margaret, my first name is Larry, you can get my family name when you agree to a date with me. Although, it is obvious from the laughter, you already know who I am. The joke is on me at the moment."

"Yes It is. Now will you answer my question or are you going to let your food get cold? Holding it this long is getting uncomfortable."

"I will take that from you and happily answer your question with a positive, YES, I am a Bomber pilot I would be honored to escort you on a date-with me-not them, just me and you."

"Here is your food, my phone number is written on the napkin under your burger. I only work here on the weekends, and I am off schedule during the week to attend college studies."

Margaret then handed off Larry's lunch and as she turned to walk away, Larry heard her say.

"Do not waste any time before you decide to call me fly-boy, I like you already, and I might change my mind and my full name is on the napkin, now enjoy your food. WHILE YOU ALL WATCH ME WALK AWAY."

Larry's friends were in simultaneous agreement as each one in turn expressed their warning to refrain from any delay in contacting Miss Margaret or he would face severe consequences of losing any chance of being with her. As for the food and beverages now consumed, Larry declared he was accepting the challenge and retrieved the soiled napkin from the plate of empty food, glancing at the phone number and her name written in a stylish handwriting. Her name was Margaret Adams. Reading the name several times before gently folding the napkin placing it in his wallet for safe keeping.

It is now Sunday afternoon; Larry decides twenty-four hours is enough time passed for Margaret to either change her mind or she should be awaiting his call. Reaching around to retrieve his wallet, he opens it to reveal the napkin had deteriorated from food stains and a sweaty wallet. Some of the numbers scribbled on the light paper were illegible. Quickly thinking of a trick, he saw on an old TV show; he went to a lampshade to hold the napkin up against the bulb hoping the light would reveal the two faded numbers he could not make out.

With the phone number now clearly visible he picked up the receiver and began the process of sticking his finger into the old rotary dial desk phone, being certain to select the correct number he dialed Margaret. A few rings later Larry was greeted with a deep older man's voice that startled him for a brief moment as he quickly hung up the phone. Thinking to himself; this cannot be the right number, did he dial it incorrectly,? did he see the wrong greasy number under the lamp's bulb?

Once again Larry went to the lamp to check the number and dialed a second time, once again making sure each number was carefully selected. Another two rings then came the same manly voice answering the phone. Larry was still puzzled the person answering was not the beautiful wait staff from the beach front bar. Quickly he decided to ask for Miss Margeret. A moment of silence passed as the gentleman who answered did not reply. Again, he asked, but this time his request came with her full name.

Broken Sanity

"Sir, is Miss Margaret Adams present?"

"You want to speak to my daughter? Came the swift deep reply."

"Yes sir, If I may sir."

"You must be Larry that dam flyboy she told her mother about?"

"Yes sir, I am."

Another moment of silence as Larry waited for a response, and his fate from Margaret's father.

"Hold on while I go out to the pool to tell her you called, she is out there with her mom talking about you."

Larry heard the receiver being placed on the stand next to the phone. The next sound he heard was a set of glass sliding doors opening as Margaret's father began calling for his daughter.

"Margee! that dam flyboy is on the phone; do you want me to run him off or can you two ladies stop gossiping long enough for Margaret to come in to talk to him?"

Margaret responded cheerfully to her daddy's announcement, as both Margaret and her mom shared a giggle together.

"I am coming in daddy, give me a second to wrap a towel around my waist."

Margaret was now inside at the end table next to the sofa, reaching for the receiver and sitting on the sofa in one gracious move she answered with a nervous voice.

"Hello! This is Margaret, is this my Bomber pilot?"

Broken Sanity

Margaret heard Larry bursting into laughter at her way of answering the phone.

"You sound like a telegraph operator Margaret."

"My apologies Larry, I admit, I am a little nervous. I was not expecting your call so soon, although I hoped you would have the bombs, I mean balls to call me."

"Well Margaret Adams, I am calling. So, if you are willing and free tomorrow evening, would you accompany me for a night out in the town together? I can pick you up around seven O'clock."

"That sounds fantastic. Did you see the address on the napkin also?"

"Yes, I did, although the phone number was smeared from a greasy burger, I managed to get it dialed correctly, see you tomorrow at seven, Margaret Adams."

"Ok, By now."

Margaret and Larry, together waited for the other to place their respective receivers on the phone base. Neither wished to be the first to disconnect from the other, listening to each other's breathing into the receiver. A minute later, and without speaking another word they both simultaneously lowered their receivers to their base, ending the call.

Immediately after hanging up, Margaret turned and raced past her father, out the sliding door to her awaiting mother. At the other end of the phone line, Larry performing the same task with his receiver, repeated the same motion of turning away from the pay phone at the barracks to see his comrades in arms all standing behind him awaiting his report.

Broken Sanity

With precision military style they all stood in respect with the required salute to another ranking office. Larry began to address his troops, trying to answer all of their questions..

"Enough questions boys, I have a date tomorrow night and that is all I am reporting for now. More information will be shared as I progress with Miss Margaret. Now begone with all of you, back to your assigned duties."

Standing by the pool, Margaret's mom was thrilled to learn her daughter had met a decent man and hugged her joyfully. Just then Margaret's father walked up beside her, taking her hand with intentions to express his thoughts and concerns.

"I would not be a good father to you Margaret if I did not give you the speech every father gives his daughter about boys. Although in this case I know in my heart you are more prepared for this journey than most women your age. So, I will forgo the standard lecture at this time, all I will say to you is, I am happy for you, and I hope this works out and when the time is right for you, your mother and I will be happy to meet him.

"Thank you daddy, you are the best."

Larry pulled into the driveway of Margarets home. Shutting off the powerful 454, big block engine powering the chestnut brown Chevrolet Nova. Opening the driver's door to step out while retrieving a bouquet of flowers he began walking up the steps to reach the porch and the front door. Instead of greeting beautiful Miss Margaret, the door opened revealing her father, standing in the doorway with a manly look on his face, large muscular arms folded across his chest. Larry now stood face to face with the head of the household. Immediately he began to sweat as he contemplated dropping the flowers and run back to his car.

Broken Sanity

"You must be Larry," asked Margaret's father, while extending his arm to greet Larry with a gentleman's handshake. I am Bruce Adams, Margarets father. Most people call me 'Big Bruce' You can refer to me as Mr. Adams."

Larry shifted the flowers to his left hand as he extended his right hand to grip this giant palm submitted to him.

"Yes sir I am," replied Larry as he reciprocated the gesture with a firm grip. "I can see why they call you Big Bruce."

"I can tell you had a good father."

"How so sir?"

"That grip you just used to shake my hand. Your father must have taught you how to great a man."

"Yes sir, he did, my father instilled his advice on this very subject, including my education and my current military training."

Margaret's father filled the entrance to the home, not budging an inch, it was now a manly stare down to see if the young Larry would flinch and run as the Florida sultry heat began taking a toll, beginning to sweat increasingly as time passed. His mind pondered what the correct protocol should be to gain-entry into the home to meet the woman he came for.

Just then Larry noticed a small petite hand appeared from behind this big man, the main sentry, protecting the entrance and the prize behind him. Larry watched the hand appear as it was gently placed on her father's waist, with a slow but deliberate motion coupled with her gentle word, "Daddy," Margaret's father graciously bowed his head, stepped back away from the doorway as he gave way to his daughter, disappearing into the house. Larry experienced firsthand the power this petite woman possessed. With a gentle touch she was able to move a mountain out of her way, revealing herself to Larry.

Margaret looked up at her date with the same beautiful smile, revealing the same bright teeth when she was face to face with him at the beachfront bar. With her gentle voice, asked.

"Are those flowers for me?"

Larry stood silently speechless, as if he had been struck by the Florida lightning, slowly raised the flowers he had been holding with the same strong grip he used to shake her father's hand, he replied.

"Yes, I thought it would be appropriate to bring you a bouquet of flowers."

"Thank you Larry, you are a gentleman. Please come inside where it is cooler and meet my parents. Margaret takes Larry's hand to escort him into the living room of her home where her father was seated in his favorite chair.

"Have a seat on the sofa next to daddy while I get a vase for these flowers."

Larry remained standing in the middle of the room watching Margaret walk into the kitchen to retrieve the vase. When he heard a deep voice say.

"Sit down son, I am not going to bite you."

"Yes sir, thank you sir."

Larry is now seated at the end of the white sofa near Margaret's father and deliberated how to begin a conversation with this huge man when Margaret's father started the conversation first.

"So, you want to date my daughter do you? Well, let me lay down some rules."

Before the conversation could continue, Margaret and her mother entered the room. Once again This big man succumbed to the power his petite daughter had over him as he quickly became silent as she informed him.

"Daddy, that speech will not be necessary, Larry has already shown me he is a gentleman."

Placing the flowers on the coffee table, Margaret introduced her mother, Lucynda, to Larry.

"It is a pleasure to meet you Larry, you can call me 'Lucy."

Margaret once again takes control of the family meeting.

"You have already met my father, so, without further small talk, mom-dad, Larry, and I have reservations at a restaurant downtown Tampa.

"Daddy, do not wait up for me, I am a grown woman and can manage myself just fine."

Larry stood up from the sofa simultaneously as her father rose to his feet. Larry once again extended his hand for the formal goodbye, glad to meet you, sir handshake and found it necessary to affirm to Margaret's father he would safely return-his daughter at a decent hour.

"You better young man, I have guns."

Margaret yells out; "DADDY, please."

Margaret reaches out for Larrys hand to save his dignity, walking him out the front door down the steps to the awaiting vehicle. Opening the passenger door like a gentleman should, Larry glanced back at the house to see Margarets father and mother peeking out the bay window of their home, awaiting their departure.

Dating a Bomber Pilot

Larry planned ahead and reserved a table for two at the Causeway restaurant. On arriving, Larry found a parking spot close to the front door. Like a gentleman he exited his side of the car first, then walked around to open the passenger car door for Margaret, gently holding her hand to help balance his date as she exited the Nova. Immediately Larry felt uneasy, the moment of meeting her daddy made him so nervous, he realized his forgetfulness to ask Margaret if she liked seafood or was allergic to shellfish.

"I must apologize Margaret I forgot to ask your preference regarding seafood."

Margaret turned to Lary and replied; "Oh please I can eat anything, and right now I am starving, Let's get inside and eat, I happen to love this place, the devilled crabs are delicious."

"That makes me feel better, actually I have never been here, it was a recommendation from my friends. I am sure you remember them."

"That I do, Larry, it was a day I will never forget. I hope that is not a warning to run now ad save myself?"

"No Ma'am, I would prefer you stay awhile."

The two love birds were now seated at a cozy table overlooking Tampa bay. The sun had just set over the horizon and the last remaining rays were reflecting off of the clouds.

Margaret looks out over the water at the mesmerizing sunset. A tear forms under her eyes as she grabs a napkin, removes her sunglasses to gently soak up the falling moisture, taking extra care not to smear her makeup.

Broken Sanity

Larry notices something is not kosher with Margaret and quietly asks, "is something wrong, Margaret?"

"No Larry, not at all. It is this 'moment,' here with you, this romantic scenery, no one has ever bothered to ask me out to dinner in a setting like this. I have never felt this emotion before now; it is a wonderful feeling I have at the moment."

Larry stretches his hand out across the table to provide comfort by holding Margaret's hand.

"This is a special moment for both of us. Margaret, I have something to say….

Before Larry could finish his sentence, the two hear the boisterous wait staff interrupting Larry's thoughts.

"Can I start you two love birds off with something to drink?"

Larry had no choice but to pull back his arm to reply, "Can you give us a moment please? We just sat down."

"Sure, Loverboy, I will be back to check on you later."

With the wait staff now gone, Margaret looked directly into Larry's eyes, with her gentle voice she asked.

"What were you about to say Larry before she interrupted our moment? Please continue."

Larry tried to muster the courage that quickly faded with the interruption. Reaching out once again to hold Margaret's hand. His thoughts nearly became words when!

"Hey, are y'all ready to order now?"

Broken Sanity

Larry could not believe he had been interrupted twice now, before he was able to reciprocate his feelings to Margaret on their first date. He replied to the wait staff and to Margaret.

"Please give us another minute, I guess my thoughts will have to wait for better timing. We should order our meal; our wait staff is getting impatient with us."

"It is ok with me, I can hear your thoughts later, on our walk along the beach."

"Margaret, are you taking control of this date? I have not asked you to marry me yet. Although I like your style of taking charge. I myself am in charge of men all day, this will be a welcome change for me."

"Maybe you should reconsider by running now and save yourself the grief."

"Are you kidding, I would never see myself as a quitter. I am here for the long haul, so get used to it sweetie."

"Correct answer Larry. We are going to make a great couple together, and maybe a beautiful baby someday."

"I like the sound of that, But let's not rush the family, we have a lot to learn about each other first."

"Agreed. So, Larry, what is your job in the Air Force, are you really a Bomber pilot?"

"I am a pilot."

"Do you fly the B-47 Stratojet or the F-84 Phantom twos?" I have questions Larry, please be specific."

"Obviously you know your aircraft."

Broken Sanity

"Yes I do Larry, I grew up here and see them flying overhead often. I have always wanted to see the inside of one."

"Well Margaret today is your lucky day, I happen to be good friends with the nightshift gate guards on duty tonight, I am sure they will look the other way for me this time. Although sneaking you onto the base could get me in trouble. The planes are always on standby anyway. I can escort you into the cockpit, where you can sit in the copilot's seat. Unless you would rather go on the beach walk?"

"Say no more Larry-we are going inside a bomber. I have to admit you just Achieved something no other man has achieved before you."

"It is just a bomber, what did I achieve with you no one has been able to do before?"

Margaret began to giggle while displaying her big, beautiful smile as she spoke to Larry.

"You silly man. I am excited and wet. That usually does not happen walking on the beach, but just the thought of seeing the inside of a US Airforce Bomber put me in gear Mr. Bomber Pilot."

Larry nearly choked on his food when Margaret revealed her situation to him. This bold articulate woman has captured his interest like no one he as dated before. Larry was comfortable being with Margaret, it was an immediate connection. Sitting across from her at the table, he watched her lips form words as she spoke fluently, never stumbling, her sentences were perfectly structured. A testament to her parents and the college education she was securing.

At that moment Larry could not help himself as he rose from his seated position, gently helped Margaret stand with him. grabbing her waist with both hands, pulled her in close to kiss her for the first time.

"I am sorry Margaret I do not know what got over me. If I am out of line please tell me."

"Actually, Larry I was wondering when you would grow a set of manhood and kiss me." By the way, that kiss was the best I have ever had. If you keep that up Mr. Bomber Pilot you might get lucky someday. After we are married of course. My daddy would kill you if he knew anything was happening before we got married."

"I can respect that and your wishes. Honestly, I would not want your father to dislike me for any reason, especially for that reason."

"Great Larry we have a deal then, we will continue dating and getting to know each other better and when you feel you are ready, You can pop the question, although first, you have to ask daddy for my hand in marriage. It would be the right thing to do. He would respect you a lot more if you did that.

"I like the plan Margaret, now let me pay our bill, we have a bomber awaiting our arrival. Before we go you have to promise you will refrain from touching anything inside the plane's cockpit."

Margaret smiled her beautiful, brilliant smile at Larry as she asked with a sultry voice.

"I cannot touch anything while we are in the bomber, are you saying everything is off limits to me?"

Larry failed to catch on to Margarets thinking as he replied to her.

"For the time being, yes, Margaret. I know your intentions are to test my resolve."

Broken Sanity

"This is why I like you Larry, you see through my playfulness. Pay the bill Loverboy so we can get out of here. I want to see how you drop your bombs."

Larry had no idea what Margaret meant by that statement. He knew it was time to escort her onto the base and into the cockpit of a massive U.S. bomber.

An hour later, Larry and Margaret arrive at the guard shack to MacDill A.F.B. Showing his credentials to the two men assigned to the gate, Larry received a formal military salute to an officer when entering a military installation.

Margaret was snuggled up close to Larry, silently taking in the sights of the Air Base as she mentions.

"I have never been on an Air Base Larry; I am so excited. Where are those bombers?"

"Patience my sweet girl I am driving us to the hangers where they are stored."

Arriving at one of the hangers, Larry stopped the Chevrolet Nova at another guard gate. "We have to walk in from here Margaret."

Larry had barley spoken his words when he heard Margarets passenger door open, she had already exited the vehicle. Larry quickly exited the driver's side to catch up to Margaret who was already walking toward the doorway of the hanger. "Whoa, little lady, slow it down," reaching for Margaret's hand to control her pace. Some one hundred yards later, the two were now standing at the side door of the huge hanger, Larry stopped and turned to face Margaret and said,

"Please promise me you will not touch any buttons, switches or levers inside this plane."

Broken Sanity

"I promise to be a good girl Larry, now can I see the bomber?" Please, Please, Pretty Please? I, have wanted to see these planes up close all my life."

Larry no longer delayed her request as he opened the hanger door for Margaret in his gentlemanly fashion. Before he could get the door fully opened, Margaret's excitement overwhelmed her as she dashed in ahead of Larry. Entering the hanger Margaret finally came to a full stop. There it was, under bright illuminating lights, the plane she desperately wanted to see. In all its glory, silently parked in full display, right in front of her, was the power of a U.S. Air Force B-47 Strato-jet bomber.

Larry walks up behind Margaret placing his arms around her waist, laying his head on her right shoulder to ask:

"What do you think of this?"

"It is much bigger than I imagined."

Playfully Larry responds to her words.

"Well Margaret, no woman has ever said that to me."

Knowing what Larry meant she replied.

"Tone it down for now Larry, I will make that judgement at a later time, I promise you that."

"I will accept that promise when you are ready, now let me take you inside this beast."

Margaret could hardly contain her excitement as she hurried up the flight of stairs to the open doorway. Once inside the mighty fortress, she began asking questions as fast as she could speak.

Broken Sanity

Larry did his best to calm Margaret, as he reminded her of visiting the plane or talking to anyone about her visit tonight was forbidden.

Margaret agreed in principle to assure Larry she would keep as quiet as a mouse regarding her experience. Then approached Larry with open arms she quickly wrapped them around his shoulders to engage in an enthusiastic kiss. Releasing Larry from her arms she shouted out.

"Larry, this was my first kiss with you inside a bomber."

"I will make note of that for future reference when I tell our grandkids."

"I like your way of thinking Larry. Now where is the cockpit? You know where the pilots sit when they are in control of this behemoth?"

"Come with me pretty lady, follow me. Please, I must reiterate. Do not touch anything."

With a playful salute Margaret replied,

"Yessir Captain."

"Lead the way Larry, let's get this show started. I want to see every inch of what you have here."

"Please Margaret, you do have a way of choosing a foray of words. I will show you everything I can show you, although there are some systems I cannot show you that would be a breach of our National security protocol. Please respect the procedure I have to follow."

"No problem Larry. Now where is your cockpit? You promised I could sit in the copilot's seat."

Broken Sanity

Larry grabbed Margaret's hand in his and lead her to the front of the plane through the opening she could see the massive console of switches, gauges, and levers.

Larry pointed to a chair and before he could say this is it; Margaret had climbed over the console to make herself comfortable. Grabbing the headset she asked Larry.

"Can we talk to each other with these on our head? I want to hear your voice in my ears. Say something sweet to me in your best pilot voice."

Margaret placed the headset over her head, securing them tight to her ears, waiting on Larry to convey sweet thoughts to her.

Larry followed suit and turned on the power to enable two-way communication with Margaret.

Margaret heard Larry's voice begin the testing.

"Test, test, can you hear me?"

"Yes very clear."

"Alright my pretty date, you are now seated in the best bomber of the Air Force. This is a B-47 Strato jet strategic bomber with six jet engines slung in pods below backward swept wings, it is capable of a top speed of almost six-hundred miles an hour with a flying range of four-thousand miles and is capable of delivering a nuclear payload anywhere in the world, with other weapons and numerous other options."

"Oh! Larry you are getting me excited, talking about this plane. You sure know a lot about it. I wish you could take me flying in it someday."

"Unfortunately, I cannot do that. Margaret we need to get off the plane and out of this hanger before the guard makes his next routine inspection and we get caught in here."

"Ok, Larry I guess I have seen enough for tonight's visit. Let us get out of here before we get caught, I am sure you would not enjoy explaining this situation to your commanding officer. Especially when I coerced you into showing me the inside of this plane. I do not want you to get in trouble and it is getting late. Let us get out of here asap."

Sitting in the dark

Larry escorted Margaret out of the hanger and back to his Chevrolet Nova, just in time for the night watchman's return security check of the hanger door. Waiting for the security detail to enter the hanger, Larry started the engine and slowly eased the car out of sight.

Once they were safely off base Larry asked Margaret if she wanted to stop at a late-night dinner for a cup of coffee and more conversation.

"Of course I would love to. Replied, Margaret. "I am not ready to go home anyway. I will be bombarded with question from my parents the rest of the night. No pun intended."

"Ok then, I know a place not far from here."

Larry drove off the main road into the parking lot. It was getting late, and the restaurant was not busy. Quickly securing a parking spot, Larry exited the car with such excitement, without thinking, headed towards the restaurant's front door, then stopped in his tracks, remembering he forgot his gentleman's duties of opening the passenger door for his date. With a perfect military-style 'about-face' maneuver, then he marched to the passenger door where Margaret was diligently waiting on Larry to grab the outside handle and open the car door.

"You almost forgot me mister. I must have some influence on your brain function. I have heard how you men lose control of your brain when a pretty lady is present. I do remember hearing something about your brains going South. Thank you for now confirming that theory."

"My apologies Margaret, I did get carried away for a moment. Let us have a laugh and be thankful I did not get inside and seated before my brain functions returned."

Broken Sanity

Margaret giggled with Larry for a moment until the car door was closed then grabbed her man with both hands, throwing him against the passenger door pinning him while thrusting her body against him and passionately kissing him.

Releasing her grip and stepping back to take in Larry's expression and posture. He was shell shocked. Still leaning backwards against the car door, she asked.

"Do you want another kiss or are we going inside for coffee?"

"I, I, well yes, inside, coffee yes we are going inside for coffee."

"Larry! Stand up, put your brains back up in the head on your shoulders and walk me inside."

"Yes Ma'am."

Larry stood up as he collected his thoughts. Then reached out for Margarets hand to escort her to the door of the dinner. Once inside and seated, Margaret greeted the wait staff and with a swift reply ordered two coffees for herself and Larry.

As the waitstaff left the table, Margaret asked Larry. "I am sorry, Did you want to look at the menu first?"

"I, I mean, we can order after we get our coffee and chat for a minute, no need to rush things."

"Great, I like your style Mr. bomber pilot. Hey Larry, I have an idea."

"What is on your mind Margaret?"

"If you are ok with it, I would like to give you a nickname. That is special to me, I know you already have some macho man call sign your Air Force pilots use to specifically refer to you when you are flying, but I have a new one."

"A nickname? Pray tell what name would you like to use to refer to me?

"Instead of Larry, I am going to call you 'BOMBER.' How does that sound?"

"If that is the name you choose for me then I can accept it. From now on you can call me 'Bomber' of course I may have to let all the other pilots know my new handle the need to use while communicating over the radio."

Margaret chuckled for a second, leaned in towards Larry, her big smile changed, then sternly requested Larry to expressly inform everyone that she selected his new call sign specifically.

Larry had no choice but to unconditionally agree to Margarets request, then noticed her smile quickly reappeared. He felt comfortable making this beautiful woman happy again. It was their first date and his only chance at first impression.

"How is your coffee Margaret?" Larry asks.

"It is the best coffee ever, Bomber."

"This new name you have portrayed on me will take some time to accept."

"Well get used to it. I will be using it from now on."

Broken Sanity

Larry picks up a menu while replying, "I like it already, Our waitress is returning, what would you like me to order for you?"

Margaret looks up at the young lady standing at their table holding a pen and order pad. Before she could ask the question of what would you like to eat, Margaret spoke with the authority.

"I will have two eggs over medium, a side of cheese grits and whole wheat toast, I am assured my boyfriend will have the same, am I right Bomber?"

Larry was speechless, but again he was on his best behavior and did not want to change what she had ordered for him and silently nodded his head in agreement. Thinking to himself, this is new for me. I have an assertive woman handling everything I do. Thinking this will be a welcome change from being in charge of others while on active duty.

Their order is now placed on the table. Larry and Margaret continued sharing details of each other while consuming coffee and food. The night was slipping away fast. Neither of them looked at a clock to check the time, when Larry decided it was past time to return his date home safely to her parents' house.

Back at the passenger door it was now Larry's turn to initiate a romantic kiss before opening the passenger door, but before he could make his move Margaret once again grabbed him with both hands and thrust him against the door, while saying,

"Come here Bomber, I want another kiss before we leave this place."

Larry happily obliged his date, then opened the door, watching her slide over to his side of the bench seat to be next to him. Starting the big block engine in the

Nova, Larry put the car in gear beginning the final leg of date night.

Larry cut off the headlights to the car as he pulled it into the driveway of Margarets' parents' house. Easing the car door open to allow his prize exit he slowly closed it, lessening the noise of the old vehicle. Taking Margarets hand to walk her up the steps to the front porch, the once again embraced each other for one last enthusiastic kiss.

Unlocking lips but remained with arms around each other, Larry looked over Margarets shoulder to see her father sitting in a wicker chair at the far end of the porch. Not wanting to startle his date he held her close, whispering in her ear.

"Your father is in the chair at the end of the porch watching us."

Quickly releasing from Larry, Margaret spun around yelling "DADDY, what are you doing out here? Go back in the house, I told you not to wait up."

"Sorry my daughter, your mother and I were getting concerned, you had not returned. It is a lot later than you normally stay out."

Margaret's father walked up to Larry and shook his hand while under a muffled voice said, thank you for bringing her home safely." Opened the front door and disappeared into the darkened house again.

Returning to Larry, Margaret embraced her Bomber once again, wrapping her small arms around his neck, she softly whispered, "now where were we."

The sun was nearing the Eastern horizon as Larry and Margaret released from each other. Larry turned to walk away; no light was necessary to see the steps below him as the sun's brilliant rays were now lighting his way.

Broken Sanity

Reaching the driver's door, he heard Margarets voice shout out,

"Good-bye Bomber, have a safe drive back to the base."

She then opened her front door to step inside, only to be greeted with both parents awaiting her entry.

In unison both parents said, "BOMBER?

"If you two must know, Bomber is now his nick-name and official call sign when flying. It was my idea, and he likes it."

Margaret momentarily turned away from her parents, then turned back towards them to say,

"Just so you both know, I plan to marry that man and have his baby."

Margarets father spoke first as his daughter was now heading to her room.

"Does he know about your plan, little lady?"

"He does not at the moment daddy, but he will soon enough. Now good night to both of you. I am going to bed."

"You mean good morning my daughter, the sun is rising up already."

From her bedroom door Margaret replies, "Nothing slips by your daddy." As she closes her bedroom door, changes into her nightgown, then slips under the covers to rest her body and lay her head on the pillow to fall asleep.

Broken Sanity

As the door to Margarets bedroom closes with a resounding click. Both parents turn to each other to address the situation.

"Well Lucy, how do we handle this?"

"We?" asks Lucynda. "It was you who sat up all night waiting for her to come home. I am going back to bed."

"Ok then, good night. Wait, good morning, no it's-neither. Go woman I am right behind you. We, yes I mean 'we' can address this at a later time."

The two parents enter their bedroom as Lucynda brings up a past memory as they begin to pull back the covers of the bed.

"I am sure she knows what is best for her. I do remember a stout younger man taking me out to dinner one night back when we were dating. If you remember we did come home quite late that night. I think the only thing holding my father back from beating your ass was you were twice his size."

Sliding under the covers, Bruce leans into Lucy and plants a well-deserved kiss on her lips as he remarks.

"Thanks for reminding me, I guess I was just like Larry back then."

Lucy whispers under her breath as she leans over to turn out the lamp next to the bed.

"I hope not."

Lucy begins to wake up. As she turns her head to look at the old alarm clock that they have had sitting on the nightstand since they were married, she sits up quickly realizing it is now six O'clock in the afternoon. Turning her head toward Bruce, she sees he is already out of bed and somewhere in the house. She smells the smoke from the barbeque grill out by the pool. Bruce always likes to cook ribs on the weekend, which means she is off of kitchen duty for the day. A smile comes across her face knowing he will also clean up his mess, he does these things for me as she rights herself on the side of the bed.

Slipping on her robe, she heads for the shower instead of checking on her man. Her mind begins deliberating. He's got this, I am cleaning up.

Out of the shower, it is Sunday, and it is also a no make-up day, no bra day. Out of the closet comes her flowery sundress. The one Bruce likes the most on her. Once again she has a plan later on for Bruce.

Opening the sliding glass door to the pool area. Lucy walks up behind Bruce to wrap her arms around his waist. Being the big man, he is, her short arms barely contact each other.

"How did you sleep my darling? Asks Bruce once he confirms his wife had come up behind him.

"Not well, although I was tired from staying up late with you and worrying about our daughter.

"Let us both hope this boy does not jump off the bridge like the last guy."

"Now Bruce, I do wish you would let that go. Margaret had no part in that boy's broken sanity."

"Mums the word my dear. Mums The Word! I should not have said anything like that. Please accept my apology"

"Do not let it happen again big boy, you do see what I am wearing? If you know what is good for you, you will keep quiet about that incident."

Broken Sanity

"I do see you are wearing my favorite sun dress and by the looks if it, that is all you are wearing. We have a deal my love."

"Great, now get those ribs off the grille, I am starving."

"Coming right up."

Sitting at the dinner table, Bruce brings in the ribs. The rest of the meal had already been prepared. All that Bruce needed to do was retrieve them from the refrigerator.

"What all did you make while I was sleeping Bruce, I see potato salad and sweet peas. You have been quite busy mister."

"Nothing but the best for you my dear. Bon' Appetite."

34

Two of a kind

Margaret rose from her bed. The air in the house was filled with the smell of fresh barbeque and like her mother headed for the shower first then to the dining table to join her parents.

Margaret exited her room and walked into the kitchen where her parents were finishing their portion of barbequed ribs.

"Daddy, I hope you made enough for me, I am starving."

"I always do. Help yourself. You know I cook something good every weekend. By the way when are you inviting this new man into our home so he can taste my cooking?"

"In due time daddy, I need to get to know him first. The last two relationships I rushed into quickly and as you are well aware those two made poor choices in their life.

"Now Margaret, your father and I were discussing this earlier and we both agreed to not address those in front of you. Although if there is anything you need to discuss we are here for you."

"Bruce spoke up.

"Even though I promised not to discuss this at our table or in this house ever again. Everyone has some concerns how two men dating my daughter met am early demise. One after the other."

"Just what are you implying daddy. You and I both know more than you've told mom.?"

Broken Sanity

Lucynda quickly lashed out at Bruce.

 "Bruce! Not today please!"

"I agree daddy not today, please!"

"Ok but, I will need to have a talk with Larry before you two get further involved."

Margaret and her mother exploded simultaneously at the sound of Bruce's last statement, both blurting out the same words at the same time.

"WHAT! WHY?"

"I guess, I need to remind the both of you, this family went through an extensive interrogation process form the local authorities. Thank goodness our names were spared from the news media. That was mainly because I have good friends still working with the law enforcement divisions I worked for."

"Well, daddy, I always said you would be the one who would know how to get rid of a body in this town. You have investigated enough crimes over the years; you should be an expert on how to do it. Right Mom?"

"I cannot believe what I am hearing from my daughter."

Lucynda continued to add more with her 'two-cents' to the conversation.

Broken Sanity

"Your daughter has a point Bruce. You do have the expertise to get rid of someone you do not like, and I remember you did not like either one of those boys."

"You are joking with me, are you not?"

"Of course we are darling. Your daughter and I have full confidence those two men must have been up to some no good. someone did what they did to them because they were broken men and off the sanity charts."

Bruce looks over at his daughter waiting on her to reply. All he received was a blank stare from her cold eyes as she looked up from consuming the meat from a large rib like a carnivore. A dribble of barbeque sauce oozed from her lips, dripping down her chin. She showed no emotion towards the conversation. Just a blank stare at her father. She knew everything and chose to say nothing.

Turning his attention to his wife, he witnessed the same nonexistent emotion towards the two gentlemen they were discussing and were no longer living. In all the years of being a detective, he looked for these clues of behavior from hardened criminals. Being void of emotion portrays the hatred one has for the individual they hurt, molested, or killed.

These signs are significant enough to warrant further or more extensive research into the individual suspected of a heinous crime. Although he knew these two boys well enough. Bruce had the resources at his department to covertly track them both just in case they stepped out of line with his daughter.

Bruce has an uneasy feeling come over him as he ponders one final question in his head before he decides the conversation should be changed.

'Do they both suspect his involvement?

Broken Sanity

Margaret asks aloud.'

"Daddy, can we change the subject please?"

"I second that." said Lucynda.

All three looked up from their respective plate of food. Everyone had barbeque sauce on their lips.

Bruce breaks the silence.

"Anyone need a napkin?"

Just then the laughter erupts as each of them reached towards the middle of the table to retrieve a new napkin to wipe the barbeque from their face.

Later that evening Margaret and her mother pour each of themselves a glass of wine then walk out of the sliding glass doors to join each other by the pool to gossip.

"Come outside and join us daddy. You surely would be interested in hearing about my date with Bomber. He showed me the inside of a Strato-jet or whatever they call those big planes."

"Who is Bomber? I though you went out with a guy named Larry?"

"I gave him a nickname. Daddy, come out and sit with us."

"No thanks, I am going into my study and watch some football. You go spend time with your mom talking about boys. I really do not need to hear all that nonsense."

Broken Sanity

Bruce closed the sliding glass door behind his daughter and watched intently to make sure both women were settled in their seats when he turned away and walked to his study.

Now sitting at his desk, he reached for the hidden key from under his desk drawer. The only key available is to unlock the bottom file cabinet. Opening the drawer, Bruce reached down with his large hand to retrieve an unmarked file folder filled thick with paper.

It was a copy of the case files on the two men that had dated his daughter. He began flipping through the file as quickly as he could. He did not want his daughter or his wife to walk in and discover he had the file in the house.

Combing through the mass of paper, looking over the investigative information used to process the case. He needed to be sure nothing was written in the file that may have been overlooked by detectives. Searching for evidence that would put himself, his daughter, or his wife in proximity to the two men. Bruce read testimony from eyewitnesses stating they saw one was being pushed off the skyway bridge and the other pushed by someone into an oncoming semi-truck. All of these witnesses had recounted their statement when it was proven they were nowhere near the crimes when they happened.

His thoughts went wild again as he was thinking to himself.

The audacity of some people, making up stories just to get their name in the headline papers or on a talk show.

Hearing the glass door to the pool area begin to slide open, Bruce quickly closed the folder and shoved the file back in the cabinet drawer just as Margaret entered the study.

"Daddy, I thought you would be in here working instead of watching football. You have never been able to fool me. What were you looking into now. A couple of your old case files you've never been able to solve?"

"Well, yes and no. But mostly yes. I agree, I have never been able to fool you when it comes to my backlog of work."

"You are retired from the force daddy, let them go. Enjoy your life for a change. Nobody in this family went to jail. No one is going to solve all those cases, and you know why."

Bruce rose from his seat when his daughter entered the room and stood at his desk with an ashamed look on his face, his head hung low. Answering his daughter with a few nods instead of a verbal response. No words were needed to be spoken between them.

"Good, now daddy relax and watch some football. I am getting my mother and myself a refill. You are still invited to come outside in the cool air and join us you know. If football is boring."

Margaret turned to walk out of the room. Bruce waited again for the sound of wine glasses being filled in the kitchen and for the glass door to open and close, concluding he was once again alone in his study. He began to mumble under his breath.

Broken Sanity

"If you only knew my child, what I have had to do to protect you from them. If you only knew what I know."

Staring back at the bottom file half closed. He pondered if his daughter suspected something. Not taking any more chances tonight he reached down to straighten out the few papers that prevented the cabinet door from closing in his haste to do so.

File cabinet now closed, and lock secured, he returned the key to its hiding place. With a new piece he taped the key to the underside of the main drawer of his desk.

Looking out of the glass door once again he was convinced the two gossiping females sitting next to the pool were engaged in conversation no one could break into. Joining them outside was not his place. He would just sit and listen to boring gossip. Standing still at the glass doors and looking out through the glass he could hear the words forming in his mind..

"There is nothing I would not do to protect them."

Walking back to his desk he picked up the receiver to his desk phone, using the rotary system with the numbers stored in his head. Bruce dialed his old friend, and the new captain of the homicide department he retired from.

"Evening this is Captain Luke Pedronia, how can I help you?"

"Luke, Bruce Adams here. I figured you would be working late as always. Listen, captain, do you remember our conversation a while back concerning those case files on the two boys that were dating my daughter when something happened to them?"

"Yea, I sure do, what is on your mind?"

"I need you to pull those files for me and have them on your desk tomorrow morning. I want to look them over one more time."

"No problem, I should have copies made and ready for you around ten O'clock, although instead of old evidence, I think you will be interested in seeing the new evidence we are looking into instead of taking home a bunch of paper, so, I will see you tomorrow."

Bruce slowly lowered the receiver to the base. It made the 'click' disconnecting the open line, then he sat down in his office chair, reaching for the remote control searching for the Bucks game.

A few hours later he was awakened from his sleep by Lucynda telling him to get up and come to bed.

"I must have fell asleep watching the game."

"You always do old man, now come to bed."

Climbing under the covers and kissing Lucie good night, his head barely touched to pillow when Lucynda asked the question.

Broken Sanity

"Were you in your office looking over the case file of those two boys again? I thought you told me the case was closed?"

Bruce had no answer to give Lucynda except for a simple nod of his head and in a faint voice he replied.

"Yes."

A few moments of silence passed before Lucynda rolled away from Bruce. As she reached out to pull the cord to shut off the bedside lamp. Once again in a low whisper she replied.

"There is nothing you are going to find in those documents. Leave it alone Bruce. Leave-It-Alone."

The lamp's bulb goes dim as she finishes her statement.

Bruce lays silently beside her, staring at the ceiling in the dark room, until he falls asleep.

Broken Sanity

Tampered Evidence

Morning finally arrived at the Adams household. Walking into the kitchen Bruce could smell the breakfast and coffee Lucie was preparing.

"Good morning my darling. I am not hungry for breakfast today. I plan to go to the station and meet some of my friends. We may go to brunch somewhere. But I will take a cup of coffee for the road."

"BRUCE ADAMS, sit down and take a breather. I know exactly what you are planning to do at that station. You are not fooling me. Like I said last night, leave it alone, we have been over this several times. We gave our statements and that's that."

"I have to make sure there is nothing in those files."

Lucynda cuts him off.

'I know, I know. Do you think you or anyone else who investigated these two crimes have any clue who the mystery persons were with both incidents? What new evidence do you think you are going to produce since the cases went cold?"

"I am not looking for additional evidence, But I have been informed there is something new the department is looking into."

Lucynda is in a shock with Bruce's statement entering her ears.

Broken Sanity

"Then what is it?"

"You know how much I love you and Margaret. You will have to trust me."

Lucynda turns away from Bruce as he comes up behind her to wrap his arms around her waist giving her a loving hug. She leans back into her man's embrace and whispers.

"Promise me you will never tell Margaret what you know or will find out. No matter what the outcome is. I do not want my daughter knowing what really happened and who did this to those two boys."

"You sound like a criminal making a confession my darling. I will leave you with your thoughts. See you sometime after lunch."

Bruce released his wife. His head filled with the only thought that came to mind.

"If only she knew. The truth."

After releasing his wife from his embrace, he gives her a pat her back side as all men do. Turning away grabbing his truck keys from the nail on the wall in the kitchen heads for the door and exits into the garage.

Hearing the truck engine start Lucynda watches Bruce back out into the empty street and drive away. Quickly placing her coffee mug on the kitchen island, she checks to see if Margaret is still sleeping in her room, then enters Bruce's study.

Broken Sanity

Walking into the study she locates the file cabinet she knows Bruce stores his cold case files in. Discovering it is now locked, she blurts out.

"Dammit!. He never locks this file drawer, what is he hiding from us?"

Lucynda decides against taking any action to mar the file cabinet. She could not take the chance Bruce suspecting she tried to get into it forcefully.

Her husband was a great detective. He would surely figure out she had been in the study and the file cabinet or made some attempt to enter it. Leaving it as is, was a safer bet for now and avoiding a confrontation later.

Standing for a moment she stared at the locked cabinet, she hears Margaret rustling from her bed. Leaving everything as is, she walked out of the study into the kitchen to greet her daughter Margaret with a fake smile.

"Would you like some breakfast my daughter? Your dad left in a hurry so, there is plenty to eat."

"He is back on the case of my two boyfriends isn't he? What is he trying to gain from his efforts this time? I thought he took care of everything already?"

"Now honey I really do not think I should discuss it with you, I know how it upsets you."

Margaret was now sitting at the kitchen table holding her mug of coffee with both hands trying to warm them when she replies to her mother's statement.

"Not as much as you think Mother. They deserved what they got, I believe something like that is referred to as, KARMA?"

"My dear, what are you talking about?"

"It is nothing worth mentioning mother, they are gone now. Are these cases closed or not? Dad cannot leave it alone for some reason. I suspect if someone found out who really pushed Carl off the bridge or who pushed Randy in front of that semi-truck. I know daddy would not hesitate to intervene in the process. I bet he would turn himself in if he himself could not produce an alibi."

"There will come a day when he will step on the wrong side of the rake and get smacked in the face with the handle."

"I am shocked you say these words to me. Please stop I do not want to hear another word about this. We have all been thoroughly questioned regarding the incidents, including your father. Now sit quietly and I will bring you some breakfast. Some decent food might change your attitude for the rest of the day."

"Yes mother I am sure it will."

Bruce Adams arrives at the Tampa Bay Public Safety office. Parking his truck in the assigned visitors' spaces instead of his old, assigned space felt weird to him. As he walks up to the front door of the station. A gentle grin forms on his face upon entering the building he spent thirty-five years of his life in. Greetings, handshakes, and conversations from old comrades temporarily held him up from the mission he came for.

With the 'how are you doing greetings' completed Bruce found Captain Pedronia sitting at his old desk. Lightly knocking on the door frame with the knuckle of his index finger notifying the Captain of his presence.

"G-morning Bruce, I see you've made it back to the scene of the crime."

Handshakes between old friends are special as Captain Luke Pedronia rises from his seating position, steps out from his desk to engage in a handshake, and a man hug with his old boss Captain Bruce Adams.

"Good to see you my old friend. How is retirement life treating you? Have a seat unless you are in a hurry."

"No, I am not in any hurry Luke, I have a few minutes to catch up with you."

"Good, lets chat a while and then I will show you the new evidence our new detective has procured. I am sure you will want to know everything we have and to answer your question before you ask. We are still working on solving the case. I have not let you down. So, with that said. How is the family? Especially Margaret?"

"Both my wife and daughter are doing fine. Well, except Margaret sometimes she has her moments. In all, she is doing her best in maintaining her sanity, given all she has been put through since the last boyfriend's demise. That second investigation did put her over the edge. She recently started seeing a new guy from the Air Base. He is smarter than the last two."

Jokingly Captain Pedronia makes a statement with a boisterous laugh.

"Let us hope he does not meet the same fate as the others."

Bruce holds his emotion inside and replies.

"You never know what will happen to anyone at any time. That is something I learned being a detective. You never know how life can turn on you."

"I definitely agree with that, no argument from me."

"Now can I see the latest information you have discovered? Who is the lead person on the case? I want to meet him today."

"Absolutely, By the way it is a her not a him. Now come with me to the video room."

"Video? Did you say video? When did you discover there was video evidence?"

Bruce's stomach began to churn. That uneasy feeling he has seen too many times from criminal interrogations has now overwhelmed him. He needed to see the video. ASAP!

Broken Sanity

"Calm down my old friend. It is not the best cinematic quality. It is on an old VCR recoded tape. I will let her explain it all to you."

Again, Bruce Adans questions.

"Her?"

"Our new recruit, she is an eager beaver. No pun intended. She actually asked to be assigned to the investigation of the first cold case when she first started working here at the department."

"Why is she so interested in these two cold cases? Explain how does that make sense."

"Walk with me. We have a whole new division now, dedicated to looking into video evidence of crimes. She found some old tape recordings of the bridge and a few recorded tapes from a teller machine across the street from where the other boyfriend was pushed off the sidewalk into the Semi truck."

Bruce walked with nervousness. He had never experienced this feeling with himself in all the years of being a detective. Matching Captain Pedronia stride, together they walked down the hallway to the building's elevator. Entering the opening doors a button was selected for the fourth floor.

Stepping off the elevator the two men took a short walk down another hallway to a high security door, Captain Pedronia retrieved a small card from his front pocket that had the four-digit security code embossed on it. Pressing the numbers in correct sequence the electronic door lock buzzed loudly as the electronic actuator released the bolt from its secured position allowing Captain Pedronia to turn the handle and open the heavy security door.

Walking inside the room with his successor. Bruce Adams was clearly amazed with the massive amount of video screens mounted on the wall with several officers pecking away at computer keyboards to control the videos displayed on the screens.

Captain Pedronia let his old boss take a moment to view the room. It was his first time seeing this innovative technology. Bruce Adams walks around the room taking it all in, then stops to look at his friend with a smile to say.

"You have come a long way from when I was here last. This will profoundly change the way the department investigates crimes. What did you bring me in here to see?"

"Come, let me introduce you to corporal Michelle Stevens, fresh from the academy. She has a degree in cinematography."

Bruce is the first to say.

"Hello corporal. It is a pleasure to meet you."

"Oh, Captain Adams it is my pleasure. I have heard so much about you. You are quite a legend around here."

"Please, let us not get into all that you have heard about me. I am humble at the moment. My friend and your captain mentioned you have a video of the crimes in the two cold cases regarding my daughter. Can you show me the evidence you have acquired?"

Broken Sanity

"I sure can, give me a minute to load the video onto the screen. These computers are new and do take some time to load up the data."

A few minutes pass as corporal Stevens pulls an old VCR tape properly label 'bridge' from a stack of other tapes on a counter next to a number of rack mounted tape players. Selecting one not being used she prepares the old VCR tape to play on the screen in front of the two men.

"Here we go Captain Adams, I have it on the screen now. As you can see, well barely, the video recording is at night at about three am. To give you some background on the tape recordings, the city of Tampa installed these cameras a few years back with the intention of watching traffic problems and or hurricane damage to the bridge. As you know they also needed to have video of any incident from the high number of cargo ships passing under the bridge. It was developed as an early warning to travelers after the sunshine skyway bridge disaster.

"Sir. Look at the screen now. You can see a vehicle stopping on the bridge. It has its emergency flashers turned on to alert any traffic coming from behind it. The two occupants exit the vehicle. They begin to quarrel or actually continue an ongoing argument at the edge of the bridge railing."

Captain Bruce Adams shifts into investigation mode for a moment. It has always been his training as a detective to ask questions pertaining to an investigation. He is quite nervous this evidence is his smoking gun when he asks.

Broken Sanity

"Can you tell from the video who this is? What type of car? Can you get the license plate number from the video?"

"Unfortunately, we cannot. These tapes are old. They have been stored in a musky cabinet in a building near the bridge where the recording equipment was housed. If I may continue, I need to show you what I see happening."

Receiving that small amount of information from corporal Stevens. Bruce Adams relaxes and continues to address the young recruit operating the computer.

"Yes of course, please continue."

"As I mentioned the two occupants are now at the edge of the railing. A few cars pass them without stopping to get involved or ask them if they need assistance."

"I fully understand that corporal. People do not care about others anymore; they mind their own business and stay away from other people's problems."

"Again, Captain if I may continue?"

"My apologies, please continue."

"It is a man and a woman. As you can see the man just stands there as the woman is obviously yelling and pointing her fingers at."

A moment of hesitation consumes corporal Stevens. Then she continues with a short apology.

Broken Sanity

I am sorry sir; the man's name is Carl we know who he is at this point in the investigation. Watch this part closely. She turns and walks away from him. He then turns his back to the parked car and leans on the railing of the bridge."

"Seems normal to me. Is he taking a breather from the argument? Or what?"

"Sir; This is where the situation changes. Do you see the other car pulling up behind their stopped vehicle?

"I see that. Is that a good Samaritan stopping to lend assistance?"

"Not at all. Watch what happens. The guy who is leaning on the railing is not paying any attention to his surroundings. The second car door opens, and a larger person gets out of the passenger side and runs over to the leaner, then pushes him off the bridge. Then calmly looks down the bridge at the female who is out of the camera's range and calmly walks back to the vehicle as it drives away. It is obvious to me there are two people in the second car. A driver and the passenger who got out and committed the crime.

"Amazing, what happens next corporal?"

"The strangest thing. Margaret walks back to the spot where her companion was pushed over the railing, she takes a quick look over the side, then looks around as if she were looking for witnesses. Then steps back to her vehicle and drives away. A more concerning problem is that this tape confirms your daughter witnessed who did it and she never called for help. She just drives away."

Frantically, Bruce Adams requests.

Broken Sanity

"I would not jump to conclusion young lady. Please tell me how you acquired this tape and how did you even know it existed corporal, and who else knows about this tape?"

"My boyfriend works for the city's bridge's maintenance department. He was tasked with cleaning out the storage locker of these old tapes. They were set to be destroyed because the city was changing everything to a digital camera system. He remembered the dates of the incident, so he kept them for me to look at before he destroyed them. We now know exactly what happened to the young man found by an angler floating in the bay a few days later."

"Thank you for your time corporal. Let us go back to your office Luke. We need to discuss a course of action."

"Gotcha. See you later corporal, keep up the clever work corporal. Let me know when you get the A.T.M. tape and begin reviewing the bank surveillance video from the other incident. We need to find the underlying cause of this as quickly as we can to close this case for good."

"All over it, Captain. I told you I will work as hard as I can until we find the perpetrator of this crime."

The two men exited the video room. As the thick security door latched behind them, they walked back to Captain Pedronia's office. Once inside and sitting at his desk. Bruce Adams closed the door behind the two men.

"What is on your mind Bruce? You look perplexed by what you just saw."

Broken Sanity

"It is not so much what I saw in there, but why is corporal Stevens so intrigued by this case? I sense she has a connection to it. What is driving her motivation?"

"Bruce, this cannot leave this room for it may compromise any conviction if we get to that point."

"You know me well enough Luke, I would never compromise an investigation to the point this department would fail at securing a conviction."

A moment of silence filled the room. Captain Luke Pedronia was the first borne son of Cuban immigrants. He leaned back in his comfortable office chair, interlacing his fingers as he stared into his friend's eyes from across the desk.

"That boy found floating in the bay was her older brother. When she reached the minimum age requirement and graduated from High school she entered our first responder youth program, then signed up for night courses in criminal justice with a major in cinematography. She made a promise to her parents to join the force for the sole purpose of finding out the truth and bringing closure to her parents."

"I understand now. When those parents found out their son had perished the way he did, it must have broken their sanity. You and I have seen a lot of broken families in our careers."

"Agreed, Now if you will excuse me Bruce, I have a backlog of cases to work on."

"Thank you, please keep me informed of the progress."

"Have an enjoyable day Captain, you too Captain.

Captain Bruce stands up, pulls up his jeans to reset them from sitting too long, reaches for the door handle, and looked back at his old friend to say.

"Would be a shame if that tape were somehow lost, tampered with or thrown out of court. Make sure it was procured in the correct manner. You know how lawyers can get evidence thrown out for the smallest of details."

"Go home Bruce, I will take care of this from now on."

A Delicate Conversation

Bruce hit the open button on his garage door opener attached to his visor when he turned toward the house from the main roadway, drove into his garage and turned off the engine while closing the garage door behind him. Stepping out of the truck he took his time to walk around the front of the truck to the entry door leading into the kitchen.

Closing the door behind him he could see his wife Lucynda standing a few feet away from him, arms crossed with a stern look across on her face. A moment passes as the two stand idle staring at each other. Bruce knows what is about to happen. The empty bottles of wine were a dead giveaway. She was ten feet tall and bullet proof.

"Lucy, please, darling can we talk peacefully about this?"

"I may have been day drinking my darling, but I am not mad at the moment. I want you to tell me what your plan is. Your daughter is genuinely concerned about you and this fetish you have to continue investigating the cold case about her and her boyfriends you never liked anyway."

"I know the both of you are concerned, not just Margaret. We have to have a conversation with her. Some new evidence has been acquired by a new recruit and the department has a new unit investigating video surveillance tape of the bridge, including a bank ATM machine video showing the street corner where the other boyfriend met his demise."

Broken Sanity

"BRUCE ADAMS, you said you had taken care of everything that could link us or her to those incidents. Let me get this straight. New evidence is being introduced to reopen the cases? What happened to you, you had our backs on this? How are you going to tell Margaret? Better yet when are you going to have that conversation with her?"

"Lucy, please calm down. Where is our daughter by the way?"

"Larry picked her up about an hour ago. Lunch date I assume. Bruce, He is a really nice young man, Margaret likes him a lot. So, let me add something to this delicate conversation we are having. You had better not say a word to him about her past boyfriends. If he finds out too soon he will be running for the hills or flying one of those bombers to the other side of the country to get away from her. I do not want our daughter to answer question about this to anyone. Have I made myself clear, Bruce?"

"Do you think you are the only one wanting all this to go away? As far as I knew it was finished. I only go in that office to check and make sure it stays that way. Although today's visit made it clear we have a problem. If she has not regained her sanity by now. This information will clearly destroy what little our daughter has left."

"What did you see on that video Bruce?"

"Lucie, you know I cannot discuss that with you."

"You Always say that, and all the other statements like, It is my job, I cannot compromise the case, or you are not allowed to know the details. I am your wife, and this is about our daughter, Bruce Adams!"

"Please trust me."

"OH! How many times in the past have you said that to me? Bruce, right now I am losing trust very quickly.

I will say this again, you better take care of this before Larry finds out."

Lucynda turns to walk out of the kitchen. Once she is out of sight, Bruce lowers his head for a second to look at the keys still being held in his right hand. Raising his head he turns to slowly position them on the hook beside the door to the garage and walks to his study to sit and digest the information he received today.

Sitting on the nova's solid bench seat, Margaret snuggled up next to Larry, when she asks.

"How fast will this Nova go Larry? What is the top speed you have exceeded over the speed limit?"

"It does have a big engine and a lot of power. I have yet to put it to the test."

"Do it Larry, I want to experience the power of this machine. You did mention it has a big engine. Show me what you have. Floor this baby for me, I need some excitement today."

Broken Sanity

"Ok let me get on the Interstate and I will open it up and show you how fast it will go."

Larry turns onto the onramp to Interstate four crossing the state of Florida. Conservatively he accelerates to eighty miles an hour and holds it at that speed.

"Come on Larry don't be a wimp; I know this car has a lot more horsepower left in it. Give it more gas Larry. Get me excited."

Larry could not resist the intimidation from Margaret to press down on the gas pedal. He dearly needed to please his girlfriend and learn for himself at what speed his car is capable of producing.

Larrys foot pressed the gas pedal closer to the firewall. The needle on the speedometer began to climb high and higher as it reached one-hundred miles an hour and climbing. The daredevil in him and the no nonsense speed he knew all too well from flying military planes was no surprise to him. He showed no fear as the car reach one-hundred-twenty-five miles an hour.

A quick glance at Margarets smile gave him the confidence he needed to press harder on the pedal. He could tell she was enjoying the thrill of the speed they were travelling. Before he could say anything to her, the sound of sirens and the flash or blue lights behind him changed his momentum.

Decelerating the Chevrolet Nova to a stop on the shoulder of the interstate. He watched the trooper with one eye in his rear-view mirror exit his patrol car while Margaret had her arms wrapped around him kissing him on the cheeks.

Broken Sanity

"Please stop Margaret I am in trouble here. I have to talk to this trooper."

"Ok Larry, I will stop for the moment."

Margaret releases her arms from around Larry and before the State Trooper steps to the driver's window she uses the opportunity for one quick grasp of Larrys manhood with her hand. Causing Larry to almost jump out of his seat.

Whispering in his ear she said.

"Don't worry Larry I will make you a happy man when we are finished with the State Trooper."

The State Trooper seeing the quick motion in the driver's seat reached for and unholstered his service revolver pointing it at Larry, demanding to see his hands, and ordering him to exit the vehicle with his hands in plain view.

Larry quickly turned to look at Margaret. She was giggling at the situation. Larry was nervous. It was the first time someone had intentionally pointed a gun at him.

The voice from the trooper repeated loud and clear.

"STEP OUT OF THE VEHICLE, NOW!"

Larry opened the driver's door slowly while exiting with his hands in the air. The next command came from the trooper with more authority.

Broken Sanity

"STEP AWAY FROM THE VEHICLE, SIR"

Larry steps away from the car door as commanded, just as Margaret leans out of the open door to greet her friend with a smile and a wave of her hand.

"HIGH TOMMY"

The State Trooper lowers his revolver and replies.

"Hello Miss Margaret, I did not know it was you in the car. How is your dad?"

"He is simply fine; this is my boyfriend Larry. We were testing out his new car. Isn't it a beauty?"

Larry is still standing a few feet away from them, who are obviously friends and have now engaged in complimentary conversation. He asks.

"Can I lower my arms now?

Trooper Tommy replaces his service revolver into the holder on his belt while replying to Larry.

"Yes of course you can. Larry, let me be clear. If it was not for Miss Margaret or me knowing her dad. I would be handcuffing you for a free ride to jail. Now get this young lady back home at a decent speed. If I catch you doing this again I will not be as kind to you as I have been today. That speed is dangerous. If her dad finds out."

Margaret quickly interrupts as she steps out of the car. Now in full view of Trooper Tommy. In her sweet southern voice, she addresses Tommy.

"That is enough Tommy. I told him to slow down but he insisted on showing me how fast this car could go. Now are we free to go?"

Without Larry noticing Tommy gave Margaret a wink from his eye as he turned towards his patrol car. Blue lights are now turned off. He drove away.

"Margaret, why did you tell him it was my fault?"

"Because I could, and if daddy finds out I had anything to do about this he will have some stern words to say about it. I cannot have my dad thinking I made you do this."

Dejected Larry concludes it is better to go with the logic of Margaret rather than argue about the situation. He figured he could restore his sanity at a later time.

Margaret steps back into the Nova, motioning to Larry to follow. Starting the engine, it roars to life and Larry steers it back onto the interstate, remaining silent about the incident while driving back to Margarets house. A couple of miles from her residence she breaks the silence in the car.

Broken Sanity

"Larry, I promised you I would make it up to you. Turn to the right at the next dirt road it dead ends by the river."

Larry complies with Margarets request while remaining silent. Finding the end of the road indeed proved to be a dead end overlooking the river. Coming to a complete stop, Larry switched off the ignition. The big engine had become silent when he heard Margaret make one more demand.

"BACK SEAT LARRY, NOW!"

At Margarets command Larry turns around and crawls over the front seat to position himself into the back as Margaret was right behind him.

Now laying together in a moment after intimacy Larry felt the urge most men feel. He was in love for the first time in his life. The overwhelming feeling consumed him to the point where he turned his head to kiss Margaret one more time before declaring.

"Margaret my darling I think we should discuss getting married if we are going to continue doing this."

"Doing what Larry?" She asks in a joking way.

"Roll over and I will show you exactly what I am saying. It is time for round two."

"I am liking you more than ever now Larry. You know you have to ask my daddy first."

"I can deal with him later, let's have more fun for now."

Larry and Margaret arrive back at her home as Margaret opens her car door herself to walk up the front staircase to the front door. Leaving Larry behind to catch up with her. Entering the front door, Margaret's mother was standing in front of her.

"I was coming to greet you. What have you done Margaret?"

"What do you mean mother?"

"It is your hair, coupled with the look on your face. I know that look all too well by now young lady."

"Just can it mother, Larry and I are in love, and we are getting married. I need a shower. Please entertain Larrry until I get back out here."

Margarets mother turns to look at Larry standing just inside the foyer of the house. He had no immediate response for Margaret's mother. The cat was out of the bag. All he could do was stand still as he waited for the hammer to fall on him. Margaret had left him in a delicate position he did not know how to handle.

Lucynda stared him down, crossed her arms in a show of force against the situation. Larry had no idea what fate he was about to encounter. There was one thought rushing through his head. He was clearly thankful Margarets father was not the first one to hear the news from his daughter.

Broken Sanity

Larry was seconds away from pulling the pin on the grenade when Lucynda became Lucie. Un-crossing her arms to reach out and give Larry a hug. Her stern face turned into a smile as she voices her acceptance.

"Welcome to the family Larry. I think you will make Margaret a great husband. Now let us hope she is not pregnant. Her father will kill you if she is. Come into the kitchen, Bruce is eating a sandwich. I can fix you one if you are hungry?"

Lucynda takes Larry by the hand and leads him into the kitchen. Have a seat next to Margarets father while I make you that sandwich.

"Thank you Mrs. Adams but I am not hungry. My stomach does not feel well at the moment."

Margarets father looks over at Larry.

"I hear you met Tommy today."

Hearing Bruce 's statement. Lucynda asks.

"Oh! that is so nice. Tommy grew up with Margaret although he was a couple of years older than her. He lived a few doors down from us. Joined the State troopers after he graduated from the police academy. Bruce was his mentor and inspiration to follow a career in law enforcement. Tommy did not have a father figure in his house growing up. Where did You meet that cute blonde haired, blue eyed, big strapping young man anyway? He is always assigned to the interstate roads. Did Margaret properly introduce you to him?"

Bruce breaks up Lucynda's questioning by putting her in her place.

"Lucie, you are interrogating the boy. Leave it alone. I can see he is nervous, rest assured he was properly introduced all right. After meeting Tommy I can understand why he has a sour stomach. Do you have something on your mind young man?"

Lucynda could hardly contain herself as she excitedly says.

"Larry has something to ask of you Bruce. Go ahead Larry ask your question."

"Well sir, I would like your permission to marry your daughter."

Bruce leans back in his chair, takes one more sip of iced tea, then crosses his arms, with a not so surprised look on his face he stares into Larrys eyes when he asks.

"She gave you some in the back seat of that Nova, didn't she?"

"Now Bruce that is not a kind thing to say to Larry or about our daughter."

Broken Sanity

"Do not acted so surprised Lucie, You did the same thing with me right before I asked your father if I could marry you."

Lucynda had no response to Bruce's memory. She fell silent, lifted her glass of tea from the counter, took a sip while turning away from the two men, it was now man to man talk time, She knew to leave them alone to figure out their next move and work out the details.

The two men engage with each other in meaningful conversation regarding the sanctity and commitment of marriage. Bruce grilled Larry extensively on his future with the service, to include what his plans were to secure a place for the two to live.

Larry did not have a plan in place at all. He knew he love Margaret. Conveying to her father his thoughts that he could not see living without her. His only plan at the time was to marry her and figure out the other details later as they go along.

Bruce tried a subtle approach to talk Larry out of his decision. Asking him to wait until he had more time with Margaret, suggesting he get to know her better before taking this leap.

"This is what I wish to do, Mr. Adams, and I believe in my heart Margaret wants this also."

Margaret walks into the kitchen hearing Larry make his declaration to her father. She pulls a chair out from the table and sits beside Larry.

Broken Sanity

"Daddy, I love this man, I trust him to take care of me. I want to marry him and be his wife. I think you would love a grandbaby to bounce on your knee. It might settle you down and give you something to love other than that police department."

Larry was now stunned. He had not entertained the thought of children with Margaret but went along with her announcement to help secure her father's acceptance of them getting married. There was one minor problem with him being able to have children he had not found the time to discuss with his fiancée.'

"Ok then, that settles this. Larry, I approve of your union with my daughter. Welcome to the family son."

"Thank you sir, I will not let you down. I will always take care of Margaret. Should I start calling you dad now?"

"Do not push your luck so soon son. You have not been fully vested."

Margaret stands up to embrace her father. As she does she whispers in his ear.

"I have this under control daddy."

Margaret embraces her father and while she has the opportunity she whispers in his ear.

Broken Sanity

"Do not say anything about the cold cases, EVER, or you will never see your grandkids."

Pulling away from her father, she kisses him on his cheek one final time before she marched Larry to the front door to say goodbye to him.

Larry thanked Margaret for the wonderful day together as he exited to his car. Leaving satisfied with a big smile on his face. He drove away.

Unknown to him, Margaret had a dark side with alternative plans for Larry and their marriage.

She knew she was already pregnant.

Deployment

Larry succeeded in driving a short distance away from Margarets house when a state patrol car pulled in behind him. Larry did not notice when the blue lights were turned on and kept driving a short distance before he was startled by the siren blaring in his ears.

Turning down the radio as he looked for an ambulance but quickly realized he was being stopped by a state patrol car. Directing his Nova to the side of the road. He switched off the car.

Looking in his rear-view mirror he waited for the trooper to exit his patrol car and approach him. No one exited the vehicle. A loudspeaker rang out from the patrolman's car with a voice he thought was familiar to him.

"STEP OUT OF YOUR VEHICLE AND PUT YOUR HANDS ON THE ROOF OF YOUR VEHICLE."

Larry obeyed the command with slow stealth like precision. He did not want to encourage confrontation from Florida's finest, and it would all be over with soon enough. He knew he was under the speed limit and did not recognize any infractions that would give the trooper reason to act this way towards him. When the next command came from the loudspeaker.

"PLACE YOUR HANDS ON YOUR HEAD AND TURN AWAY FROM THE PATROL CAR."

Larry was now more nervous with this latest command over a loudspeaker. The Patrolman had not exited the vehicle. M<multiple scenarios were swirling in his head. Guessing what could he have done to cause this protocol from the state trooper when the next burst of the loudspeaker relayed a gentler message.

"HANDS DOWN, RELAX YOU ARE NOT THE PERSON WE ARE LOOKING FOR. NOW GET BACK IN YOUR CAR AND DRIVE AWAY."

Larry' heart was pumping hard and steady until he was commanded to relax and drive away. Larry fumbled to find the keys he had left on the seat. Still nervous he found the key to the ignition, inserted it and with a quick turn the big chevy engine roared to life.

Before shifting into gear, Larry took a glance in his rear-view mirror to see if he could identify the trooper still sitting in his patrol car. Unfortunately, he was met with the glare off the trooper's windshield and could not see the man's face.

Larry decided not to waste any more time looking in the mirror as he reached for the column shifter to put the car in gear. Now rolling away from the patrol car he took one more glance back at the trooper but still could not get a clear view of who the trooper was.

Larry finally calmed himself as he reached the barracks to change into his uniform and jump suit to go flying. Getting in the air for some time alone and a single-seater A10 Wart Hog was a perfect fit, for getting in the air and maneuvering the machine any way he wanted.

Larry was now cleared for flight. Pressing the throttle to gain speed, the plane's TF34-DE100A turbofan engines thrust the plane in the air. Directing his flying time over open water in the Gulf of Mexico, it was time to practice firing the 30MM-GAU-A8 Avenger gatling gun on pre-placed practice targets away from civilian populations to avoid mistakes.

Finishing his flight time, it was time to call Margaret. He was curious to hear how her day finished after he left for the base. Larry was concerned her father or mother would attempt to talk her out of marrying him. It was the only thing on his mind during his flight.

Changing back into his day uniform he found an unoccupied office he could use for privacy. Picking up the receiver he dialed the number to Margaret while hoping her father was not the one to answer and make small talk before handing the phone to his daughter.

He was in luck. Margaret answered on the first ring.

"Hi Larry, I figured it would be you calling. I am sure you went flying after your visit with daddy and Mother. They are excited to see you and I getting married. Mother is already engaged in planning a big wedding at our church. She has already called her friends and the pastor to confirm an available date."

"That is good news, I was worried they would talk you out of it. So, they are ok with us getting married?"

"My mother is ecstatic; Daddy is daddy, he is a man as you can tell he holds his emotions inside a lot, although he did smile at me when he left mother and I in the kitchen to work out some details for the wedding, It is what girls do you know."

"Oh, yes I am sure you two had a number of issues to discuss. To answer your previous question, I did go flying and I want to let you know. You were heavy on my mind the whole time I was in the air, even after getting stopped by another State Trooper on the way to the airfield. I am beginning to think I am being followed."

"Oh! Larry I think of you all the time, that trooper might have been Tommy. He stopped by shortly after you left. Him and daddy went outside on the porch to sit while mother and I stayed in the kitchen. Did he say hello or anything? Were you speeding?"

"No not at all. I did nothing wrong. I was ordered out of the car from a loudspeaker. It was a weird stop. Not a normal procedure."

"That is weird Larry, I cannot say for sure it was Tommy or not, but I do know he was here shortly after you left."

"If it was him. He treated me like a criminal; I did not appreciate the way he treated me."

"I will ask daddy when I get off the phone if Tommy mentioned anything. I do know he has always looked out for me in the past, although my past is nothing to worry about. We are getting married and that is that."

"Today was a great day announcing our plans and my flying time, I felt really good except when the trooper had me outside of my vehicle with my hands on my head."

"Oh no, I did not know he did that to you."

"Margaret are you holding back on something you should tell me?"

"No, not at all. I will say if it was Tommy, he was testing you."

"Why does he need to test me? That does not sound like a sane man that should be on the state's payroll."

Broken Sanity

Margaret becomes defensive with Larry's questioning and his last statement about her close friend Tommy.

"Listen Larry, Tommy is remarkably close to me, and you had better get used to it. We grew up together and he always swore to protect me. He was a wide receiver on the football team, and I was a cheerleader. We have been close friends ever since I was born. He lost his father a long time ago in a car wreck. He looks just like his father. A tall man with blonde hair and blue eyes. My mother loved that man."

"Ummmm, that is too much information for now. Please, Margaret let me apologize for upsetting you. We can talk about what you have divulged at a later date and time."

"I am sorry Tommy, I did not mean to go off on you like that."

"Margaret, you just called me Tommy."

"It must have been a Freudian slip. We were talking about Tommy, but my mind was thinking about you. It is Parapraxis error in speech that happens to people. I hope you understand I made an error, and I did not mean to say his name."

"It is a good thing you did not do it when we were intimate in the back seat of my car."

Margaret begins to laugh. Larry has defused their first disagreement. Now that he has his fiancée in a better mood, Larry changes the subject of inviting Margaret out to dinner so the two of them can discuss their life together.

"I will pick you up tomorrow night for dinner. We will head down to Ybor City and get some good Cuban pork with yellow rice topped with black beans and raw onions. How does that sound to you?"

"I like your way of thinking Larry; I will be ready by seven O'clock."

"Great, see you then."

"Hey Larry."

What my darling?"

"I love you."

"Love you too, see you tomorrow."

Larry walks out of the office with a smile on his face and joy in his heart. His life with Margaret is moving forward at a fast pace. Walking down the hallway of the command center he turns a corner and comes face to face with a young lieutenant. Stopping to salute Captain Larry he proceeds to announce that the flight commander needs to see him in his office immediately.

Larry responded with an inquiring of the nature of the requested meeting. The lieutenant could only give his senior officer a shrug of his shoulders with a whispering reply.

"I think you are getting deployed, Sir."

Larry left the young officer as quickly as he arrived with the information. Force marching to the flight commander's office. Walking past the assistant at her desk he grabbed the door handle and slammed his body against a locked door. Turning back to the assistant to watch her giggle at him and speak.

"If you will slow down I will get you in to see the commander shortly. He is on a conference call with the pentagon at the moment and cannot be disturbed."

Larry replies.

"What is this I am hearing about being deployed? Where am I going? When am I going? I have plans to get married."

"I do not have the answer to your questions."

The secretary takes a quick look at her office phone to inform Larry the commander is now off the line and will be opening the door to greet him, he knows you are coming and suggests he check his uniform before meeting the commander.

Larry takes her advice and checks his uniform for accuracy and tucks his shirt back in to his pants. In his haste to get to the office his shirt had come out of his pants. He did not look presentable to the commander.

Finishing the check of his uniform, he heard the sound of the door unlocking as the handle turns with the door to the commander's office opening. A tall well-built man with the weathered age of a solder ready to retire emerges from the office.

Larry stands at attention, saluting the bird colonel in front of him. The two men exchange proper military salutes. A necessary procedure of respect to a superior officer.

"At ease captain, come in and have a seat."

"What is this about asks Larry."

"What I am about to reveal is top secret and no one is allowed this information of the mission beyond your crew members. Do I make myself clear captain?"

"Yes sir, of course sir. Although I do need to tell my fiancé, I am leaving town."

"You have been selected as the top officer in a mission to fly a couple of bombers to the island of Guam in the Philippine sea. I am not sure of the reason; it is above my pay grade. All I know is we need additional assets in the region. So, prepare your crew. You leave a week from now. A briefing is scheduled tomorrow in the war room; more information and details of the mission will be revealed then. Make sure you inform your crew as soon as possible. That is all captain, you are dismissed."

Larry leaves the commander's office a little dejected. This hampers his plans to marry his sweetheart. Although this mission will boost his opportunity to be selected for an increase in rank, he needs the extra money and benefits it will bring to him and Margaret.

With his mind racing in every direction, he decides to wait until he takes Margaret out to dinner. First things first. His military obligations come first. Larry begins the task of alerting his crew members of the planned meeting tomorrow and they should all prepare for a deployment next week. It was a task he did not accept well and neither did his comrades.

Broken Sanity

Later that evening Larry dressed in civilian clothes and drove off the base to pick up Margaret. The long drive was a solemn one. Contemplating how to tell Margaret and her parents he was being deployed on a secretive military mission that he could not discuss with them. He knew Margaret and her mother were already in the planning stages of the wedding.

Turning off the main highway he noticed a State patrol car sitting behind a commercial building. Just as he was passing the stationary officer he observed the patrol car exit its parked position and fall in behind him. Following him to the last street corner towards Margarets house, once again he was being tailed.

Larry's eye was trained in the rear-view mirror awaiting the blue lights to come on at any minute, when he looked back through the windshield just in time to slam on his breaks to prevent hitting a parked car on the street. Heart thumping with anxiety and now relief he had made it to Margarets home and pulled into the driveway. Exiting his Chevy Nova, he looked back at the patrol car that was now stopped in front of Margarets house. He could clearly see it was Tommy, Margarets friend. Instead of walking up the steps to her house, he decides it is time for a man to man talk with Tommy and walks over to the patrol car just as Tommy opens his driver's door to meet his oncoming opponent.

Larry stops a few feet in front of Tommy allowing him to exit his patrol car. Tommy Is now in front of Larry as he dons his official trooper's hat. He is a big man. Much larger than Larry. Both men are professionals and a stare down begins. Larry breaks the deadlock with a question with a precise military voice of authority.

Broken Sanity

"Why are you always tailing me? Was it you who stopped me the other day? Yelling thru your loudspeaker to get out of the car? What is your problem with me?"

Larry takes a step towards Tommy; his fists were clinched. He wanted to punch this man in the face. Tommy places his hand on his service revolver as a precaution to protect himself if necessary when they hear Lucynda's voice ring out from the porch.

"You boys going to come inside or stay out here and dance with each other?"

Larry turns away from Tommy as he declares one last statement to him.

"This is not over with yet."

The two men walk up the steps to the house together, not showing their disgusted emotions for the other as they meet their host. Lucynda greets them both as they top the stairs. Behind her Bruce has emerged from the doorway to greet Tommy with enthusiastic respect, ignoring Larry's presence, the two men move towards the end of the porch for a face-to-face discussion.

Lucynda pulls Larry inside by the hand as she comforts him with an apologetic voice.

"Pay no attention to those two out there. It is the way they have always been. Something I live with daily.

Officers of the law I am guessing. They love talking shop. Margaret is getting ready for your date night. Come into the kitchen, would you like a glass of tea while you wait for her?"

"What I would like to know is a little more about Margarets friend Tommy. He is very protective of the occupants of this house. Especially Margaret."

Before Lucynda could answer Larry, Margaret overheard the question as she was entering the kitchen and delivered a quick stern response shutting her mother down as she shouts out.

"MOTHER! Leave it alone. I can handle this on my own with Larry I will explain it to him later."

"Thank you dear. Larry I am just a mother, but I have observed that precise look you have on your face. Do you have something on your mind? What is troubling you? I hope it is not Tommy and his attitude."

Margaret snaps at her mother.

"Mother that is not a nice thing to say about Tommy."

Larry commands the room with his next statement.

"I have some disturbing news Margaret needs to hear and for you and Mr. Adams also. Margaret you might want to sit down for this."

Broken Sanity

Margaret takes a seat while asking Larry a question with an aggravating voice.

"Are you getting cold feet? You are, are you not?"

Perplexed at Margarets assumption Larry looks at both women as he announces he is being deployed in a week to the Island of Guam. If the two of them are to be married, they need to do this as soon as possible.

The Secret Porch Society

Bruce and Tommy continue to talk on the porch while Larry delivers the news to his bride to be and her mother.

"What have you discovered?" Asks Bruce.

"I have been tailing him ever since you asked me to follow him and look into his background. The only thing I have found so far is he has a couple of speeding tickets. Other than that, he is clean as a whistle."

"I am not so sure of that Tommy, everyone has a skeleton in the closet somewhere. How did he react when you stopped him the other day leaving here?"

"I scared him so bad, I am sure he had to go clean his pants. I treated him like a criminal suspect. You should have seen him shaking when I called him out of his car over the cruiser's loudspeaker."

"I would have given anything to be a fly on his windshield during that stop. Excellent job Tommy, we do not want him to get too comfortable around Margaret. The more we can break his sanity the better off he will be. And you can have the chance to marry her. It has always been my desire for you two to get married instead of those other boys."

"I am doing my best sir. One other thing I have to inform you of. He did stop at a jewelry store on the way here. Do you have any idea why he would do that?"

Broken Sanity

"I thought Margaret told you already. He is another boy falling in love with her and he is planning to marry her. Margaret and her mother have been buzzing around here for a couple of days planning the dam thing."

"How would I know about this Bruce?'

"Come on Tommy do not act surprised at what I already know. You have been sleeping with my daughter for some time now. I have never mentioned it because I know you too well and I am assured you are using protection."

"Don't tell me she has not told you the good news."

"What news is that Tommy?"

"Nothing Bruce, I will let her tell you when the time is right for her. I know she stands up to you often on matters that concern her. She is a very strong-willed woman. But sometimes she needs to hold back on letting you know what is happening to her."

"I get that about her."

"Another thing Bruce, what is this news you have regarding new evidence in the two cold cases involving Margarets old boyfriends?"

"How did you hear about that, Tommy?"

"You did mention it yourself Bruce, you know we are still sleeping together. She was over at my house the other night. I will leave out the details of our encounters and just say she mentioned it to me. When were you going to let me in on the information the department has obtained? Do we have a problem?"

"Tommy, I am looking into it as we speak."

Broken Sanity

"What can I do to help Bruce? You know I am always available."

Bruce fills Tommy in on the video evidence that has been discovered and now in the department's possession for analysis in the new media room. Bruce also conveyed the name of the young lady, Michelle Stevens, who has a boyfriend who actually found the old tape from the bridge surveillance camera.

"I need to get his name somehow and let you know who he is. He is an employee with the department of bridges here in Tampa. As soon as I can get his name I will need you to lean on him for more information on how he acquired these video tapes. We do not need any more of them transferred to Miss Stevens for analysis."

"I am your man Bruce. Let me know when you have his name."

"There is more Tommy. A bank automatic teller machine video is being procured from a local bank. As soon as it is available it will also be analyzed. I need you to have a face-to-face talk with the banks president if you know what I mean?"

"Sure, thing Bruce, I would hate to see a bank president succumb to a mysterious tragedy. Can you find out which bank and the name of the president? I should pull him over to give him heads up. A little warning to watch his back for a while might be the order of the day."

"I am heading back into the department next week to talk to captain Pedronia. I may be pestering him too much by showing up more often than he would like me too."

"I agree Bruce, you do not want to give him any indication to suspect you as a subject of his investigation."

"I will try to remember that Tommy. Now get out of here and be safe on the streets, including your time with my daughter."

"Sometimes she only comes over for one thing Bruce. I really doubt she loves me as much as you think she does."

"That is enough Tommy get off the porch. Our conversation has ended for now. I do not want to hear any details concerning you and my daughter's late-night encounters."

Tommy turns away from Bruce producing a half-made salute to his superior. Knowing everything well enough there is always more to this story than he is being told. As he takes to the steps leading down to the driveway, his mind ponders if he should look into the circumstances of what happened to Margarets two boyfriends himself.

Bruce watched as Tommy drove away from the house. Then he walked into the kitchen where he was met with a volley of sounds from his daughter and wife as both began to speak simultaneously trying to gain his attention and let him know the current situation Larry had presented to the two of them.

Bruce could not understand both women at the same time. He raised both hands in the air and yelled.

"STOP, STOP, both of you stop talking. One at a time please. Margaret, what happened while I was out there on the porch talking to Tommy? You two ack like Bomber dropped a nuclear weapon."

"Daddy, Bomber and I have to get married right away, he just received orders today from his commander, he is getting deployed to the Island of Guam and he does not know how long he will be gone, and I cannot wait until he returns to marry him."

Tears began to roll down Margarets cheeks as she tried to explain the situation and her commitment to marrying Larry. Bruce's fatherly instinct kicked in as he walked over to embrace his daughter to comfort her. Everything he had wanted and hoped for his daughter went out the window as he caved to her request. His hopes and dream of her marrying the boy down the street crashed in an instant. Making sure his daughter was happy was his priority from this point forward.

Bruce releases his daughter as she rushes to Larry for another embrace. Lucynda and Bruce come together also embracing each other. Bruce had to make a statement to control the situation.

"Larry and Margaret if you two love each other that much. Then we need to find a justice of peace or get the pastor involved to get you two married tomorrow morning. Margaret my daughter I will make a few phone calls to expedite your marriage certificate while your mother calls the priest to see if he is available tomorrow morning?"

Lucynda tells her two lovebirds to get out of the house and enjoy your date night while her and Bruce work out a plan to make this marriage happen quickly.

Broken Sanity

"You two go on your date. Your father and I will take care of the details and let you know what we have planned when you return. If you two return tonight that is."

Larry took the lead with Margaret, leading her out of the house with his arm around her waist. Driving away Margaret snuggled in close to him on the Chevy Nova's bench seat when she begins to show her love to Larry while he is driving.

"Margaret, I have to concentrate on the road, or we may have a wreck."

No sooner did Larry express his thoughts than his eyes glanced up at the rear-view mirror on the windshield. A short distance behind them was another state patrol car turns in behind him from a side street. Larry is now aggravated and yell aloud.

"THIS HAS GOT TO STOP."

Margaret's feelings were now hurting, thinking Larrys outburst was directed at her actions and halts her embrace to move her body back to the passenger side of the seat.

"Larry, I cannot believe you yelled at me to stop loving on you. How dare you."

Broken Sanity

Still looking in the rear-view mirror, Larry was expecting the blue lights to turn on any minute.

"Larry, are you paying attention to me? Why are you mad at me?"

Larry's main focus was the patrol car closing in on him. Instead of waiting for the lights to flash he decides to pull the chevy Nova to the shoulder of the road for a complete stop. Putting the cars' transmission in park, Larry notices Margaret was now on the other side of the seat staring at him in anger. He realizes she thinks he was yelling at her instead of the trooper behind him.

"My darling, my expression was not directed towards you or your embrace. We are getting pulled over again by Tommy."

No sooner did his voice express the words, the patrol car slowed to a crawl as it passed the two sitting on the side of the road. The police officer inside was not Tommy but another officer. Although Larry and the police officer lock eyes with each other as he drove past them.

Saying it again as his head turned back towards Margaret.

"This has got to stop, Margaret, it has to stop now."

"What are you talking about Larry? What has to stop?

Broken Sanity

"This following us everywhere we go, everywhere
I go. I need to know what kind of relationship you and
Tommy have. I noticed he was outside on the porch with
your dad for a good while. Do they have some secret porch
society? I do not think your dad likes me."

"Larry my darling, can we talk about this later?
You are so stressed out at the moment. I have a plan. You
start the car and drive us to the restaurant. I will slide over
to your side of the seat and continue caressing you. After
dinner we are stopping by the river, and I will make you a
happy man. How does that plan sound to you?"

"This is why I want to marry you Margaret."

Margaret and Larry are now heading home from
dinner and the river. Pulling into the driveway Larry once
again becomes aggravated at the site of Tommys patrol car
and the two men on the porch having late night chat when
both men turn to look directly at Larry.

"Larry I see what you are concerned about, but I
want to tell you before we exit the car. Those two charac-
ters on the porch do this all the time and way before you
came into my life. It is a police thing. So, do not read anything into it for more than it is."

"Alright Margaet. I will try to remember that. Let
us go inside and see what your mom and dad planned for
us while we were at dinner."

Playfully Margaret responds.

"You mean dinner and the river. Now walk right past those two on the porch and come inside where we can find Momma. She has all the details anyway."

The two men fail to acknowledge the two love birds walking up the stairs. Reaching the front door the two men turned their backs to Larry and Margaret while lowering their voices to a whisper.

Margaret and Larry find her mother sitting out by the pool. Opening the sliding glass door they both take a seat beside Lucynda and Margaret opens the conversation.

"What were you and dad able to work out mother?"

"First of all, it was me, not your father and I. Secondly, I have everything put together for you. You two need to be at the church at noon, but before that you two have to swing by the courthouse and pick up the marriage certificate. Then your father and I will vacate the house so you two can come back here and consummate your marriage."

"What, Mom, consummate?"

"Margaret my daughter. It has to be better than down by the river?"

"MOTHER!"

"Oh, do not act like I do not know what you two have been doing. I was young myself one day. How do you think your father and I."

Margaret heard enough.

Broken Sanity

"THAT IS TOO MUCH INFORMATION MOTHER! ZIPIT."

Bruce and Tommy are finishing their porch meeting as they shake hands and exchange good-bye's. Bruce walks into the house and out to the pool area.

"Lucie did you fill them in on what these two need to do tomorrow?

"Yes I did honey, I took care of it. You can go back into the house now."

"How about Larry and I have a chat in my study and you, and our daughter can spend time together out here until we are finished. Come with me son."

"DADDY, I have already expressed my thoughts to you. Please honor my wishes."

"Your secrets are safe with me my loving daughter."

Bruce and Larry reside themselves to Bruce's study. Closing the door behind them Larry decides to be brave and blunt with Bruce. Figuring it was better to stand his ground show no fear than to be trampled by this man for the rest of the time he is married to Margaret.

"Bruce, Mr. Adams or should I refer to you as Dad? I want to know what is going on with you and Tommy and a better question I should ask is what is Margarets relationship with Tommy?"

Broken Sanity

"It is an ongoing investigation, and I cannot answer that question right now. So how about you and I take some time to get to know each other."

"I expected the typical police officer answer from you. But I am not leaving this room until I have the answers I requested."

"Fair enough, put your seatbelt on. This is going to be a rough ride. And it does not leave this room. If Margaret finds out I told you she will never let me see my grandkids."

"I agree to your terms Bruce, I mean DAD! And just for the record I have something to reveal to you as well. I hope you can keep what I have to say between us as well."

"Do not ask me to lock pinky fingers, we will both agree as gentleman to our secrets."

"Agreed sir."

Lucynda knocks on the door to get the two men's attention as Bruce walks to the door and opens it.

"What is it Lucy" he asks.

"Tommy is here to see you. He said it is urgent."

"Tell him I will be out on the porch shortly. We are about to finish in here."

Broken Sanity

"Gottcha, big guy."

Closing the door, Bruce turns back to Larry to ask one final question.

"You have all the information on my daughter I can give you. If you decide to run and save yourself I cannot blame you for doing so. So, what is it you have to tell me? Make it quick I have to talk to Tommy."

"Do not expect to have grandkids from me. I suffered a freak accident that damaged my ability to have children."

Bruce took a brief moment to digest what Larry had revealed and politely said.

"Ok, but do not be surprised at what you find out here shortly."

"What does that mean sir?"

"Nothing, I am going out to talk to Tommy now. Go back out there to the girls. I will be in shortly."

Bruce walks out on the porch to greet his friend Tommy who is anxiously waiting at the corner of the porch.

"This better be worth showing up here this late at night."

"It is Bruce."

"Go on, I don't have all night son."

Tommy hesitated for another few seconds then whispered to Bruce in a muffled voice so no one would hear him.

"I visited the branch manager of the bank today. The tape has already been transferred to the department. Instead of threatening him I had to act like I was checking on the transfer of the video tape. So, he would not suspect anything. I shook his hand and thanked him for the speedy transfer."

"That is not the news I needed tonight. Go home now. I will check on what they see on the video in a couple of days."

"Ok, If you need anything else Bruce. Let me know."

"I will. Now get off my porch."

"You are so kind to me. Goodbye Bruce."

Broken Sanity

Instincts Prevail

Captain Luke Pedronia arrived early to work on a hot sunny Wednesday morning. While sitting in his office chair he now reached for the night report that had previously been placed on his desk when his assistant knocked on his door.

"You have a visitor to see you from the State Troopers. A trooper Tommy Neelsom I believe is his name. Do you have a scheduled appointment you forgot to tell me about? He said he has questions to ask you about the Margaret Adams cold cases."

"No, I did not make an appointment with anyone, and I would never make an appointment without informing you first. I wonder what questions he has to ask us? Show him in, I can look over these reports later."

"Yes sir."

Tommy Neelsom is a tall man with blonde hair and blue eyes. He is not a man you want to tangle with when he pulls you over for a traffic violation.

Captain Pedronia's assistant enters the office with the unannounced quest and begins to introduce the two officers.

"Thank you Tammy, you can close the door on your way out."

Broken Sanity

Without another word spoken the two men engage in a handshake as Sergeant Tommy take a seat when he hears the door close behind him.

"What is the nature of your visit sergeant?"

"Thank you for seeing me today. I do apologize for showing up unannounced. As you might know I am good friends with the Adams, I grew up near them and I am remarkably close to Margaret."

"Close-Close you say. Just how close. Are you here to confess to assisting her in killing those to boyfriends?" Before you begin I will need to read you your Miranda rights and get a stenographer in here to record your confession."

Trooper Tommy was in the hot seat with Captain Pedronia. Squirming in his chair while attempting to find the correct words to diffuse the situation that was now escalating out of control. Regaining control Tommy made it clear he was not there to confess any involvement in the cases.

"Again, my apology sir, I am here to offer some information in the cases. I have an instinct about crimes. Especially when it involves someone I know."

"Calm down trooper, I am busting your balls. I know you were not involved in either case. Although I am curious what instinct you have to share with me today that might help us solve them."

"OK, let me calm down and I will let you know what I have for you and who I think could be the perpetrator of the crimes. I know you have interrogated Bruce's daughter extensively. I also know she has given your investigators little information."

"Stop right now Sergeant. Are you telling me you have inside information into these two cold cases? These files were sealed because at the time Margaret was a minor."

"Let me explain sir. I am here to help solve the cases. If you do not want my help I can leave now."

"I am listening. Let me get a pad of paper to write down your information. So, all the previous kidding aside. Are you here in official capacity as a witness to these crimes or have you been provided confidential information regarding these crimes? I am still trying to understand the nature of this visit before we continue."

"Sir, I have a hunch Margarets dad may have played a role in those two boys meeting their early demise. Does that help you understand why I am here?"

Captain Pedronia sat up quickly in his chair and looked Tommy eye to eye. He was stunned to hear his lifetime friend of thirty years may have been involved in the two murders. Now leaning back in his seat, he grabbed a tissue from his desk to wipe away the sweat forming on his forehead. His nervous system was taking over. Had his friend lied to him all these years. No wonder he mentioned something about the tapes getting tampered with. It is making sense to him.

Siting up straight again captain Pedronia angrily points his fingers at Tommy as he says.

"If all you have is a hunch. You might think twice in keeping this information to yourself until you are sure.

Broken Sanity

Because if you are wrong young man you might as well resign from the force because I will not hesitate to have your rank and badge stripped from you, young man. Now tell me what you know, I do not have all day."

"I agree with you Captain Pedronia. I hope I am wrong about this, and I should keep quiet until I do further investigation. So, I will refrain from giving you details of what I know and have heard from Bruce Adams.at the moment. Just so you know. Bruce and I have had several conversations with each other on his front porch, and he has asked me to look the other way on some activities I know about Margaret."

"Is he covering his tracks? He knows a lot about criminal mind games and regards to Margaret. That is his daughter, do not forget that sergeant."

Before Tommy could say another word, Bruce opens the office door.

"Hey Captain, where is your assistant. She usually is at her desk to notify you I am coming."

Bruce finished asking his question when he noticed sergeant Tommy is sitting in one of the seats in front of Captain Pedronia.

"What are you doing here Tommy? I thought you were out on interstate patrol today."

"Are you tracking my whereabouts Bruce? I thought I would see the new guy that took over your office. That is all."

The three men were now seated together at captain Pedronia's desk when his assistant Tammy opened the office door to inform her boss.

"The F.B.I. is here to talk to you about the cold cases. Oh, high Captain Adams I must have been in the restroom when you came by my desk. Good to see you again."

"My pleasure Tammy."

"Enough small talk with Bruce. What is the nature of his visit? Did he mention it?

"Obviously the same reason these two are here."

"Bring the F.B.I agent in here. Today is becoming really interesting. It looks like the gang is all here. Let us move over to the conference table."

The two visitors already sitting down take a moment to stare at each other. Bruce has a stunned look on his face. Hearing Tammy's remark he realized Tommy had just lied to him. Standing up they move over to the small round oak conference table near the window. Bruce and Tommy elect to sit across from each other instead of beside one another like friends. Bruce is noticeably upset and sends a glare of dissatisfaction towards Tommy. His bond with him is broken.

The Agent from the F.B.I. joins the three at the table as he introduces himself and begins to inform captain Pedronia for the reason he is visiting today.

"Captain Pedronia. The F.B.I. has been following the two cold cases since the reporting in the news and as you know we do not get involved unless there is a request for our services or an outside informant has expressed concern the local investigation is compromised."

Bruce intensifies his glare on Tommy. There is one thing he learned in all the years of being a crime scene investigator.

There is always someone sitting at the table you cannot trust, and Tommy just became that person.

The F.B.I. agent began explaining the cases in detail, what he knew, what the agency knew so far. Then he began questioning captain Pedronia about the new video recordings that were discovered showing the two crimes as they happened in real time. Continuing he requested to see the video recordings and obtain a copy to take back for further analysis using advanced technology at the bureau.

Captain Pedronia looked over at his old boss to say.

"This is great news don't you think Bruce? We may finally see who the big guy is on the recordings. If you excuse us, I will take the agent to the video room while you and your friend the trooper can leave us to our duties as public servants. Now go home Bruce, I will let you know what we find out when the time comes."

"I am afraid you will not be able to share the information with anyone captain Pedronia. The agency will now be taking the lead on these two cases. I am sorry it is out of your hands for now. I have federal court orders with me to confiscate all evidence you have."

"I see, well, unless you have a court order instructing this police department to cease and desist in investigating a crime in our community. We will be continuing to do so. Now I must say goodbye to my friend, Bruce, and sergeant Neelsom. Bruce, I think you two know your way out of the building."

Bruce and Tommy exit the police station together as they walk side by side each other out into the parking lot. Bruce is now enraged at Tommy and follows him to his patrol car.

Tommy removes his keys from his pocket. Now placing his key in the lock when Bruce grabbed Tommy by the shoulder, spinning him around to face him while using both hands shoving his friend back against the door frame of the patrol car and begins to scream questions at him.

"What do you think you are doing? Did you call in the F.B.I.? I was handling this. Now look what you have done."

Tommy regains his composure and returns the favor by shoving Bruce back away from his face. Insults and accusations were flowing in a loud exchange as a group of police officers rushed over to break up the altercation.

Knowing Bruce was their old station captain no charges or arrests were made. Bruce was now being held back by two younger officers as they escorted him to his truck.

Tommy remained behind talking to other officers assisting with controlling the situation.

Bruce started the engine in his truck, backing out of the parking space, then drove by Tommy yelling out the passenger window at him.

"I AM NOT FINISHED WITH YOU, TOMMY, YOU HAVE SOME EXPLAINING TO DO."

Broken Sanity

Tommy replies to Bruce in the same angry manner as Bruce drives away.

"I THINK YOU ARE THE ONE WHO NEEDS TO BE EXPLAINING YOURSELF."

Captain Pedronia enters the secure video room with his F.B.I. agent in tow behind him and locates corporal Michelle Stevens.

"Corporal this is, I am sorry I have forgot your name already."

"Agent Stevens, Roger Stevens, it seems we share the same family name corporal."

"Hello uncle Roger."

"I was not going to mention that small detail Michelle, but now that the cat is out of the bag, I suppose captain Pedronia needs to be informed of our connection to each other."

"No need for further explanation Roger Stevens! I see the resemblance now. So, Michelle are you the person who called the F.B.I. to get involved?"

"Actually captain, I did not call anyone. My uncle overheard my conversation with my boyfriend while he was attending a family birthday party. He began to ask questions about the cold cases. That is when he decided to get the agency involved in the cases. I felt obligated to pass on the information regarding the video and how it was obtained. That is protocol is it not sir?"

Captain Pedronia was visibly upset at the situation of losing control over a local case. Quickly realizing his department was hitting a point of no return on the time spent on the cases, he finally replied to corporal Stevens and informed her she did the right thing.

"Agent Stevens, I will need to see the paperwork from the court order on my desk before I relinquish any evidence. Surely you understand I have to follow proper protocol when transferring evidence."

Acknowledging Captain Pedronia's request the agent Stevens pulled an envelope from his inside jacket pocket and handed it to him and replied.

"I believe, this is what you are looking for captain? You are welcome to read it thoroughly. Everything is in order there."

Looking over the document captain Pedronia had no choice but to release the evidence to a higher authority.

"Right now, I need to make a phone call to an old friend and other duties to attend to. For now, I will leave you two here to discuss and complete the transfer of evidence.. I sat to you corporal Stevens, we will talk later on the proper procedures of discussing evidence outside of this building."

"Yes sir."

Captain Pedronia leaves the secure video room and closes the door behind him. Standing in the hallway waiting for him was Bruce.

Broken Sanity

"Captain Bruce Adams. What are you doing back here? I told you to go home."

"We need to talk."

"You dam right we do. Get in my office."

Bruce and captain Pedronia arrive at his office. Closing the door behind him he reaches for the string to close the blinds.

"Have a seat Bruce."

"I prefer to stand for a moment."

"TAKE A SEAT BRUCE." Captain Pedronia demands.

Bruce finally eases into one of the chairs in front of the commercial steel desk. It was never a fancy piece of furniture. Budgets were budgets and nothing changed that.

Captain Pedronia picked up his desk receiver to inform Tammy via the intercom to hold all visitors until further notice. One more thing he said.

"Get me someone in here to record this conversation."

"That will not be necessary captain."

"The hell it isn't Bruce. You sir are now the subject of interest in this case. The two videos confirm a big guy pushed those two boys. You are a big guy. The F.B.I. is taking the video recordings to their field office to enhance them. Soon enough they will be able to confirm who our perpetrator is or give us a clear idea to work with. Do you have anything you need to tell me before they complete their findings?"

"Yes."

Wedding Day

Larry showed up to Margarets home like clockwork. It was not a day he would miss of ever forget. With all the information her father passed on to him about Margarets past boyfriends and problems she has endured, he still loved her more than ice cream.

Lucynda gathered the two youngsters in the kitchen to explain every part of the details of her marriage plan. Where they should sign the documents, who was performing the ceremony, what church they needed to drive to.

"There is only one change to the plan Margaret."

"What would that be Momma?"

"I booked the honeymoon suite at the Grand Hyatt. I figured you two need a night to remember other than staying here at the house."

"Thank you Mrs. Adams that is very thoughtful of you."

"Oh, please Larry you can call me Mom from now on, I think Bruce has accepted that you should call him Dad after your chat in his study last night."

"What did he tell you about that talk?"

"I understand you two bonded quite well, He mentioned how much he admires you for joining the Airforce and your long-term goals with Margaret."

Larry could not believe his ears. This man has gas lighted his wife into believing he and Bruce were now friends. He was left with the one option. Play along, go with the flow, and say nothing per Bruce's instruction. Larrys thoughts were mixed. Should he remain silent?

Broken Sanity

Given the circumstance of marrying Margaret today. He chooses to keep his mouth shut. Surely he figured with time on his side the truth would prevail.

"Come now, the both of you need to get going. Bruce is in the garage warming up his truck. We will meet you at the church.. Larry I almost forgot to ask."

"Did You bring the ring?"

"I do have the rings. Straight out of a Cracker Jack box."

"Larry, I am not getting married to you today with a cheap ring. Please tell me you bought nice rings for us."

"Yes my love, I would not let you down."

"Fine, let's get going."

Margaret selected a white miniskirt and top for her wedding gown, complete with the seventies style white lifted open-toed shoes to complete her ensemble. Confirming with Larry he had the rings in hand she turned and walked out the front door leaving Larry and her mother staring at each other.

"Larry, I think you should follow your fiancé."

"Oh, yes, I guess we will meet you and Bruce at the church. Bye now."

Lucynda threw her arms in the air in disgust as she turns to head to the garage where Bruce was patiently waiting in the truck.

Broken Sanity

Climbing in the truck and closing the door. Bruce pressed the button on the garage door opener and started the truck. Bruce was exceptionally quiet on this day when Lucynda turns to him to say.

"I will be glad when this is over. I hope he gets housing assistance and takes her out of the country. Is it true they will not charge her if she is in another country?"

"I am nonplussed at your question. Why do you still believe your daughter had anything to do with the demise of those two boyfriends."

"It is my intuition I suppose. I know you have thoroughly investigated these cases. I also know you have refrained from telling me the truth of what you know. Honestly, I am tired of the gas lighting Bruce. When are going to come clean with what you know about the cases?"

"Lucynda, you know I cannot talk about cases like that. Besides that. I will tell you the F.B.I. is now involved and they are taking all the evidence the department has back to their field office for analysis."

"What does that mean Bruce. Are they trying to pin this on one of us? What if they put you or I in jail? I will not be happy in an orange jump suit. So, I suggest you do something about this F.B.I. agent."

"Have you lost your mind woman? I cannot bump off or as you say, take care of an F.B.I. agent."

"Ok, hear me out. There is new evidence brought in. A new recruit has a boyfriend working with the bridge department. He secured a video of the bridge the night Carl was pushed over the side."

"What, he was pushed? You and the news media said he jumped off that bridge."

Broken Sanity

"Now do you see why I could not let you know what I know. An investigator would notice you knowing that small piece of information and try to link you to the crime. So, you, not knowing he was intentionally pushed has cleared you from being a person of interest in the case already."

"Bruce."

"Yes Lucy."

"Do not say another dam word to me about what happened. No matter what I ask. Promise me you will not say another word until this is over with."

The rest of the drive to the church was silent. Bruce had already made a mistake in telling his wife a small detail she did not need to know. He also held back his conversation with captain Pedronia at the station the day before. He knew she would never forgive him if she thought he was a person they considered a subject needing further investigation.

Arriving at the church. Bruce parked his truck, turned off the ignition and sat silently for a moment staring out of the windshield.

"What is it Bruce? You seem a little broken today. Are you not comfortable with Margaret marrying Larry?"

Without saying too much to his wife. He looked over at her, leaned across the console for an intimate kiss.

Broken Sanity

"You know this is the same way we got married twenty-three years ago. I had higher hopes for our daughter when this day came for her."

"That is the Bruce Adams I married. You love her more than anything else in your life. You are the type of dad that would push someone off a bridge if it would save your daughter from a life of misery with someone you did not like."

"You know me too well Lucie. Let's get inside before we miss the ceremony."

Inside the church, Larry and Margaret were sitting with the same Babtist preacher that married them twenty-three years prior. Now gray haired with a cane for support resting against his knee. He looked up at the two approaching mother and father.

"Are we ready?" He asked.

All four simultaneously reported with a resounding echo of.

"Yes."

With the ceremony now queued. The two stood in front of the pastor to repeat the vows of matrimony.

The final magical words were now spoken aloud.

"I now present to the world Mr. and Mrs. Larry Rawlings. You may kiss your bride sir."

Broken Sanity

The two turned to look at their parents. But before they could walk away. Bruce stood up and asked the preacher a question.

"Father, do you have some advice to share with Larry before he leaves? I am sure you have the same advice you gave me the day you married Lucie and I."

"Why yes, I do remember giving you a piece of my wisdom."

With one hand of the preacher now placed on Larry's shoulder he turned to accept the advice from a distinguished elder of the church.

"Larry my son. If I can give you one piece of advice it would be this."

"NEVER TRUST ANYONE WHO NOW, HAS ACCESS TO YOUR TOOTHBRUSH."

Everyone broke into laughter. Especially Bruce. He knew this was the same advice a once younger up and coming pastor passed on to him when he got married to Lucie.

The two newlyweds walked outside with the intention of driving to the hotel by themselves. Instead, they found a limousine parked in front of the church waiting for them. Surrounding the Limo was Tampa's finest motorcycle core ready to provide a police escort to their honeymoon suite.

Broken Sanity

"Daddy you should not have done this for us. We could have driven our self."

"I know Margaret, but I wanted to give you two a better send off than your mother and I did when we were married. So, think nothing of it. I will have the Nova brought over to the hotel tomorrow. For now, all you have to do is enjoy the evening as a wife."

Larry steps up to shake Bruce's hand while thanking him for the ride and the escort when Bruce pulled him in close to whisper I his Larry's ear.

"Just so you know. I had a box of condoms sent to the room ahead of time."

"Thanks DAD! One thing I failed to tell you is I am sterile. An accidental hit on the football field in high school ruined that for me. To make up for not having any balls I became a Bomber pilot. See you later sir."

Bruce stepped back away from Larry as he watched his now son-in-law climb into the limo with his daughter. All he could do is stare at the limousine as it pulled away from the church under police escort. Larry had the last laugh on his new father-in-law.

Lucie steps up beside her husband, wrapping one of her arms around him while wiping away the tears with the other. Then she asked.

"I wonder if we are going to have a grandchild in nine months from now. Hey, What words of wisdom did you convey on our new son-in-law? I saw you whisper something to him."

"I do not think we are going to have any grand-kids Lucie. Let's go home. I have had enough fun for to-day."

Standing in front of Bruce's truck. Lucynda stops to ask Bruce.

"Why do you say that Bruce? Sometimes you can be so mean with the things you say to me."

"All I can say at the moment is you should not get your hopes up. Now get in the truck please. This is making me hungry. We did not plan for food. Unless you have dinner planned. We should go out to eat before we get home."

"Sounds good to me. I was thinking we should reenact our honeymoon night ourselves when we get home. What do you say to that big man?"

"I like your plan Lucie. Now will you get in the truck?"

"Yes dear. I love your romantic style of being forceful. Can you use your handcuffs on me again to-night? I can be your prisoner."

"Stop Lucy, I cannot focus on that and drive at the same time."

"I can get you focused on something."

"Ok, that's it. We will have to eat later. I am driving home first."

"I knew I could change your mind."

"You have a way of doing that to me."

Broken Sanity

The Wire

Captain Pedronia decides he needs to address the issue of corporal Stevens openly discussing pertinent information regarding cases at a family gathering. On his way into his office, he passes Tammy's desk with a stern request in passing.

"Tammy, summon corporal Stevens to my office immediately. I need to have a word with her."

"Yes sir."

Captain Pedronia began reviewing the nightshifts reports when he hears a lite knock with a female voice.

"You requested to see me sir?'

"Close the door corporal and take a seat."

"Yes sir. I want to say sir…"

Captain Pedronia cuts her off from speaking with a wave of his hand.

"I did not bring you in here to admonish you for what you did at a home party on your own time. To be honest with you This department needs a separate set of eyes on these two cases. We were not getting anywhere close to solving the cases and I need your focus somewhere else."

"Sir I believe, we are getting close to finding out who the person was on the bridge that night when my brother was pushed into the bay. I need to solve this for my family. It is the very reason I started this career in law enforcement. Do you understand what this means to me and my family to find closure?"

"I believe the F.B.I. will find that person utilizing the technology they possess. Which brings me to the job I want to put you on."

"I am listening."

"I want you to get out of that uniform."

"EXCUSE ME SIR!"

"As an undercover agent for the department. What did you think I meant?"

"Nothing sir. As long as it pertains to the investigation of my brother's murder, I will accept the job."

"We have not determined it was a murder corporal. Although the mission I need you for will be clear. Let me explain all the details first, then you can decide if you are willing to accept the challenge."

"It sounds interesting enough. Please continue."

"I have contacted the F.B.I. station chief asking for cooperation with the investigation. What we need is someone to infiltrate the local education facilities where Mrs. Margaret attended. Especially her high school and college campuses. I need you to covertly talk to every person who knew her. Find out who she who she developed friendships with and who she was seriously involved with, like an intimate partnership where jealousy could be a motive to make a person push your brother off the bridge and the other in front of a semi-truck."

"I follow you sir. Anything else?"

Broken Sanity

Captain Pedronia leans forward from a reclining position, placing one fist on his desk to reply.

"Yes there is. First, I need you to to wear a wire to record all the conversations with the individuals you talk to. The department has contacted Margaret's high school principal and the dean of admission at her college. You will be allowed on campus with a transfer student id to avoid suspicion. Second, after you complete the first task you will be required to mirror the movement of the previous captain that sat in this seat before me. Can you do that?"

"Is he a prime suspect sir? I know these cases involve his daughter. I also know he was exceptionally good at his job."

"My hope is that answer is a no. Although I have a duty to uncover every stone on the path to a conviction. With that being said, you are ordered to start right away. And corporal, I need to clarify one thing."

"That is sir?"

"You are to report to your uncle and to me the same findings you produce as our liaison. This is to be a joint investigation between the bureau and our police department. No one else has authorized access to the information contained in your reports and absolutely no one should be made aware of this operation, which includes your boyfriend. Do I make myself clear corporal?"

"Absolutely sir."

"Good, now get out of here and start talking to her classmates. Find all of them who knew her. You are dismissed corporal."

Broken Sanity

Corporal Stevens leaves the captain's office and headed home for the day. As the evening sun set, corporal Stevens prepared a set of questions she felt appropriate she could ask to help the investigation. There were a number of questions she needed answered, but she could not risk the chance of someone discovering she was an undercover police officer and ruin the investigation all together and decided it was best to limit her questions during her first visits to the schools. She jotted down the following reminders in her notebook.

*How do you know Margaret?

*Were you close friends with her?

*Did she ever talk about her boyfriends or the ones who died?

*Did she have any big male friends?

*Was she intimately involved with anyone?

*Any jealous men in her life?

*Did she make enemies?

Falling asleep on her couch corporal Stevens was awakened by the pounding of a fist on the front door of her apartment. Standing up she realized she was still in uniform as the pounding repeated on the door with a loud voice from a man outside yelling thru the door.

"CORORAL STEVENS ARE YOU IN THERE?"

Broken Sanity

As the voice faded from her ears she opened the door to find a male and a female officer from the covert department, each holding a briefcase.

"Why are you two here this early in the morning?"

"Captain Pedronia didn't inform you we were coming by your house to fit you with an audio surveillance wire. We were instructed to come here to fit you. He did not want to take a chance in someone getting a tip off if they saw you getting it done at the station. Whoever might give a dam and tip off someone we all know."

"Oh, yes, please come in. You are?"

The African American female officer engaged with Corporal Stevens in a stern manner.

"It doesn't matter who we are, you are supposed to be undercover, remember? Why are you in a wrinkled uniform? Did you sleep in your clothes last night corporal? Have you had a bath? You smell woman; I am not touching you until you take a bath."

Michaelle was upset at the officer's tone, but she did sleep in her uniform. Accepting her tone of voice, Michelle opened the door wider as she stepped back out of the way.

"Please have a seat. I will go take a shower before you put the wire on me."

Broken Sanity

The two-officers stood stunned with their brief-cases in their hands as they turned their heads to look at each other when Michelle Stevens silently turned away heading to the bathroom of her house.

"I told you so George. Captain Pedronia made a bad choice when he asked this woman to take an under-cover job."

"I tend to agree with you Tina. Let's have a seat. The sooner we get this done the better."

Michelle was gathering a clean set of civilian clothes from her bedroom dresser. But before she could get into the shower, she heard the female officer shout out to her.

"Call me when you get out of the shower please and leave your top off, it makes it easier to tape the wire under your tiny breasts."

Michelle Stevens takes a moment to look at herself in the mirror as the last words from the female officer were still resonating in her head. Pondering what did she just get herself into, shrugged her shoulders as she turned away from the mirror to pull back the shower curtain reaching for the faucet handle to start the shower.

Now finished with her shower, Michelle took extra care to thoroughly wash herself to prevent her coworker from mentioning any lingering body odor. As she steps out to dry herself off, she yells out to the female officer.

Broken Sanity

'I am ready, Please tell me that male officer will not be helping with the installation of the wire?"

Special assistant Tina rises from the couch as she grabs a briefcase containing the covert equipment she will be taping to Michelles body.

"Don't you worry about George, his job is to make sure the sound works when I am finished with you. So, calm down. Now turn around while I tape this transmitter to the small area of your back."

'My back? Why did I need to leave my top off if that is in the back?"

"You have never worn this before have you?"

"No"

"The small microphone is taped to the front of you under them titties you have. Now turn around and let me finish doing my job. Ok, I am done, you can finish getting dressed now then come out to the living room so George can turn it on and test it."

Michelle enters the living room and announces to George.

"Ok George, do your thing so I will be done with the two of you today."

George opens his briefcase that is filled with electronic switches and dial. Plugs in a wire connected to his headset to listen for a tone. Tina starts a countdown from ten to one as George confirms the wire is in full operation. With his dry joking voice, he declares.

"We are good to go Huston."

Both officers close their briefcases and report to Michelle, they will return tonight to download the voice recording onto a thumb drive and remove the wire, informing Michelle, they will be back daily to repeat the procedure.

"Under no circumstances are you to take this off by yourself. If we do not make it back, you are to sleep with it on,"

"You have got to be kidding me Tina."

"Of course I am kidding. One more thing, we have your student ID's somewhere in this briefcase. Yes here. Use this to get access into the college and the High school where Margaret attended. Bye now."

Civilian Michelle decided to check out the local college campus Margaret was attending. She figured it made more sense working at this venue for clues first then if she did not get any information on Margaret she would then backtrack to her high school.

Captain Pedronia provided her with some intelligence when she accepted the position. It was a list of who's who. All she had to do now was find the friends on that list.

Broken Sanity

The list was short, with two girlfriends and two male friends. Michelle had one advantage when it came to finding the two girls she was looking for.

Michelle was so glad captain Adams answered 'YES' when her now captain Pedronia asked captain Adams if there was anything he need to say at their last meeting.

He had a lot of intelligence to pass along. The man was a genius when it came to investigating crimes. His retirement prevented him from taking an active role in cold cases, and this one was personnel to him. He needs this to get resolved. Not only for everyone's piece of mind, but for his daughter to be cleared of wrongdoing.

Michelles stomach growling was an indication she was hungry. Glancing at her watch she discovered it was indeed lunchtime, and the student cafeteria was a suitable place to look for the first people on her list.

Selecting a pre-made garden salad from a glass refrigerator, she headed to the cashier. With food in hand, she began looking around the cafeteria for her first contact. There in the far corner sat the tall brunette with the scarf in her hair just as it was described to her.

"Bingo"

Rang out in her mind as she headed towards her table. Thinking this is too easy as she weaved her way through the maze of tables when she spotted a big muscular guy standing up just two feet away from her. Blocking her intended travel route.

Broken Sanity

Stopping abruptly before running into this giant man when he turns to face her. Looking down on her and producing a smile he excused himself.

"Excuse me, I did not see you coming."

Looking up while holding her salad close to her chest. Michelle could see bedroom blue eyes, muscular fore arms and flowing blondish hair. Michelle stood like a stone statue without moving. Quickly composing herself she replied.

"Oh, It is my fault I did not see you getting up. My focus was on someone across the room."

"Do not let me get in your way. I am a big guy but will gladly move to the side for you. Can we talk some-time? Let me introduce myself, I am Steve Thompson."

Michelle replied. I think I would like that. Let me set this salad down and I can give you my home number and we can talk later tonight. If that works for you?"

"Perfect. While you are at it, please print your name on the paper with the number."

Michelle nervously sets her salad on a table then retrieves a notepad from her back pocket. As she is flipping to a blank page to use to write her number on, she temporarily stops on the page with the four names she had written down for her to remember who she was looking for. There at the bottom of her list was Steve Thompson.

Tearing out the paper that now contained her name and number she handed it to Steve.

Broken Sanity

Steve looks down at the paper to read the number and the name scribbled on the paper.

"Catrina McDaniels."

Captain Pedronia suggested Michelle use an undercover name when encountering the people on the list. No one needs to know her real name for safety reasons.

Retracting her hand, Michelle reached for the salad she placed on the table then turned her body sideways to slip past the troll guarding her path. Turning her head, she said.

"Call me tonight big boy."

Now walking away, she began looking for her intended target and refraining from looking back at her new friend as she became extremely nervous when she realized the brunette had left the cafeteria while the big man was blocking her.

Michelle stopped at the table her initial subject had been sitting at. Her thoughts began running wild in her head as she sat down to think, "Was it, is it, him?" Did she just have a conversation and give out her phone number to the person who pushed her brother off the Tampa bay bridge?

"Is he the big guy in the bridge video?"

Unable to eat the salad, Michelle picked herself up while nervously looking around the room at the crowd of people minding their own business. Everyone was talking to someone. Her appetite now diminished, it was time to leave the cafeteria and for good measure to ensure no one recognizes her and tossed the salad into a trash can at the exit.

Michelle was optimistic she could find the other two named on her list before leaving for the day. A high stakes cat and mouse had already begun when she began deliberating why the big boy decided to block her way at the exact moment she was about to pass him. Was it intentional? Or a by chance?

Now outside the cafeteria, walking amongst a well-manicured courtyard with a maze of shrubbery, trees and freshly cut grass. She could see many students sitting on benches or on the grass with others studying for exams as she mumbles to herself in a low whispering tone.

"Where did they go? They cannot be too far away."

Just when Michelle ended her outdoor search, she headed for a door that would lead her into the study hall located next to the student parking lot. Quickly surveying the parked cars, she stopped. There they were both the brunette and the big boy from the cafeteria.

Embraced in each other's arms.

A Journal Entry

Bruce slipped out of bed early, leaving his Lucie snuggled under the covers. Heading into the kitchen to start a pot of coffee. His mind is still wrapped around his daughter. The wedding went as planned and Larry is set to deploy in a couple of days. All should be well in the household. He should not feel this uneasy feeling. Pouring his first cup of coffee he walks thru the sliding glass doors to sit outside to sit by the pool in the cooler morning air. Florida afternoon heat is unbearable to most people and to others it is comforting.

Bruce's mind begins to wander off as he sits alone. Instinctively the cold cases enter his thoughts. Retiring from the police force has proved to be harder of an adjustment to this new life than he bargained for. His plan was to walk out of the department and never look back on the work he accomplished for the past thirty plus years of wearing a uniform every day.

Solving case after case. Securing convictions for heinous crimes perpetrators commit with as much or as little evidence as possible. In some cases, it came down to one or two key pieces of information that solved the puzzle his department was tasked to put together. Sipping the last of his cup of coffee he realized the cold cases connecting the dots to his daughter's two ex-boyfriends' demise had a missing link no one has yet to find. He rested knowing the key piece he had hidden was never going to be found.

Another trip into the kitchen for a refill of coffee, creamer, and a spoon of sugar. A cough from his lungs shook his old, tired hands as he dipped into the sugar container, raising the spoon, another cough caused him to spill a few granules onto the counter. Prompting Bruce to reach for a kitchen towel to wipe them up before his wife could find fault with cleaning up after him. Before leaving the kitchen he noticed Lucie had left her checkbook on the kitchen counter then turned away to wipe up his mess. Disposing of the kitchen towel and the granules of sugar attached to the towel, he graciously stepped on the bottom of the trash can to open the lid. Just before depositing the spent kitchen towel, he stared down into the open trash container to see a discarded check book register.

The years of investigating all sorts of crimes kicked in hard as he quickly questioned himself and his next move. Should he retrieve it? or should he leave it lie right where it is? Staring at the check register deep in the trash he could not release the lid with his foot to make it close.

Raising his head while simultaneously lifting his foot off the pedal, he watched the lid slowly close as a thought entered his head.

"I need a therapist, here I am thinking my wonderful wife's checkbook register may contain evidence to those crimes. I am losing it."

Bruce left the kitchen heading to his study. He could not let this case go unsolved. Unlocking his file cabinet, he retrieved his folders filled with the handwritten information he collected while investigating the crimes. Finding his notepad and a pencil he opened the book to a blank page and began writing the information his successor passed on to him.

He wrote 'Video' at the top of the page. Under that 'big guy' then drew a large question mark next to both words. This signifies at this point there was no answer to who that person was on the bridge pushing Margarets boy-friend into the water.

The next two words he wrote under the previous two words were 'motive' and 'why.' Some investigator will be asking these very questions someday.

'How did he know when to be there?' was the next sentence. The video clearly indicated he had knowledge of Margarets where abouts. Continuing to deliberate in silence he wrote, 'who knew where she was?' with one word left in this sequence he scribbled, 'TOMMY' continuously using the pencil to trace out and highlight the letters of his name, it stood out on the paper in bold print.

'Tailed?'

With another question mark was his last entry. He knows my daughter to well. Could this be my fault? Bruce asked himself, I did ask him to keep an eye out for her and keep her out of any trouble. This was the provocative question to return to the upper word he wrote. 'why?'

Bruce was becoming nervous and anxious to have a conversation with Tommy as soon as possible. When he was startled by a mild knock on the door frame of his study. Bruce was deep in thought, not realizing his Lucie was standing in his doorway asking.

"I am starting breakfast do you want anything?"

Bruce replied with a resounding.

"Yes dear that would be great. Thank you I will be right there. I made coffee already."

Broken Sanity

"I see that, good boy and I see you cleaned up after yourself."

Lucie disappeared from the doorway as Bruce closed his notebook, wrapping a large rubber band around it to hold all the papers stuffed in it as he replaced it in the file cabinet. With one turn of the key his notes were safely locked away.

Walking into the kitchen Bruce sat down at the table awaiting the arrival of the fresh waffles his wife was preparing. Initiating small talk with Lucie to pass the time. He asked.

"Do you want me to get the plates or silverware, syrup out of the fridge maybe? I know you never let me do anything to help, I am always in your way when you are cooking."

"Bruce, you know this kitchen is not big enough for the two of us at the same time. So, just sit tight I will have everything served to you in a minute. By the way I do believe we need a new waffle iron, this one is on its last leg."

"Sounds about right, why don't you take that checkbook you left on the counter last night and go into town today and purchase a new double waffle iron for us. That would cut down the time it takes to make them, so we can eat them together."

"Great idea, I have been wanting one for a while. While I am gone, you can go back into your study and search for more evidence in your paperwork. Do not think for a minute I did not notice why you left our bed so early this morning."

Broken Sanity

"You read me like a book Lucie."

"Yes, albeit a broken book. Do you think you will ever find what you are looking for?"

Bruce rarely shares his information with his wife. A protocol that has stood the test of time with his marriage. Leave it at the office door and never bring home your work. This time he slipped up and without thinking he shared the newly discovered information with his wife, the department had a video of the incident on the bridge.

The words had just cleared his lips when he heard the bowl of waffle mix drop to the floor, slipping from Lucies grip as she replied to him.

"What did you just say?"

"Are you ok Lucie? Can I help clean that up?"

"No sit down, It was empty. Can you elaborate on what you just said?"

"You know I cannot do that."

"Dam you Bruce, you can but will not. I know you too well. You always keep information you should be sharing to yourself. Never mind I am going to take a shower and head out for a day of shopping. You can clean the kitchen and please take out the trash before the garbage truck gets here.'

Watching Lucie storm out of the kitchen he yells out.

"Can I have the waffles you are not going to eat?"

Broken Sanity

Bruce begins the task of cleaning up after eating the remaining waffles left in the Iron. Placing the empty waffle mix box in the trash can along with the scrapings of waffle mix from the bowl Lucie dropped on the floor before storming off to the shower. Collecting the can liner and tying the opening with a tie twist he headed out through the garage to place the bag in the bin. As he was rolling the bin to the street he heard Lucies car start up backing out of the garage down the driveway to the street where she placed in in drive leaving Bruce standing alone next to the garbage bin.

With not a single wave or a kiss goodbye she sped off to town. Bruce turned to head back to the house when his mind remembered the check book journal in the trash bag. He could not let it go. He had to have that journal. With an about face he stepped up to the bin opening the lid with one hand while reaching in with the other to re-trieve the freshly placed trash bag. With little effort he ripped open the bag searching for the journal.

Using his hand to sift thru days of coffee grounds, old food, soiled paper plates and now a handful of dis-carded waffle mix he finds the journal soaked and covered with a mix of trash.

Holding the smelly batch of paper with one hand he skillfully holds open the lid of the trash container while placing the remnants of the trash bag back into the bin.

With his prize in hand, he looks around making sure the neighbors did not see this episode of dumpster diving.

Now back in his study he proceeds to look thru his wife's check book journal. Thumbing through page after page of the same entries, grocery store, bookstore, cloth-ing store, checks for school supplies for Margaret. It was the same entries over and over again. Thinking he was off base with his actions, he continues to the last page in the journal. There it was, on the last page, in her handwriting was an entry. A large check was written out. For what strange reason would his wife have to write a check for that amount? That entry caused Bruce to stop for a moment to think.

Written on one of the entry lines was Tommy's name with the word 'PUSH' next to it. The amount entered was soiled and barely legible from being in the trash. Using a small rag to clean off the paper the entry was nearly washed out. Opening his top desk drawer Bruce reached in to find his magnifying glass to aid his aging eyes. Placing the magnifier over the journal he could make out, four thousand dollars written in faded ink.

An unsettling feeling consumed Bruce as he began contemplating the worst of the worst and questioned could this information be the link that makes sense of it all to an investigator? His next thought was the hardest one to swallow. What would an investigator link this check register to?

Did Lucie pay Tommy to push those boys into harm's way? It was obvious from the video he witnessed a larger person with a different physique than Tommy, so, it could not be him in the video.

Looking back on his notes and pointing at the word he wrote down. If it was not Tommy, 'WHO' then?

Tommy was now off the interstate and enjoying a Cuban sandwich from Brocato's when his cell phone rang. Looking at the number he knew it was Bruce as he deliberated answering the call then elected to let it ring out to voicemail. The voice in his head led him to finish his lunch before returning his call, besides that, no one needed to overhear his conversation anyway.

Broken Sanity

Bruce was persistent, knowing when Tommy was on the road and when he took a moment to have his lunch. Some people never break their routine. That he knew from being an investigator. He knew Tommy well enough to give him a moment to get himself in a position to talk.

Bruce decided to give his friend ten minutes to finish lunch. His thinking led him to believe Tommy should be sitting in his patrol car right about now. Once again, picking up his cell phone from his desk, he dialed Tommy's number.

Tommy answers on the second ring.

"Hello Bruce."

"Hey Tommy, first I want to apologize for running you off the porch last week. That was rude of me to do so."

"It was not a problem for me Bruce, I know I touched a nerve discussing your daughter and I know you can be a hot head when that happens. How can I help you today?"

"You and I need to discuss something urgently. Can you stop by the house soon before Lucie returns from shopping?"

"Consider me on the way Bruce, see you shortly."

Both men end their call to each other as Bruce walks out to the front porch, taking a seat to await Tommys arrival.

Tommy arrives at the house a half hour after their call ended, steps out of his patrol car and walks up the steps to sit next to Bruce.

"You took long enough, no blue lights to clear the traffic?"

Broken Sanity

"You failed to mention this was an emergency session, Bruce."

Without a single word spoken, Bruce lifts the check book register from his lap. A paperclip holds the ledger open to the last page where Lucie wrote Tomy's name and the sum he was paid.

Tommy takes it from Bruce; with a moment of study, he asks.

"What is this you are handing me Bruce?"

"It is a ledger from my wife's check book. I found it in the trash. Can you enlighten me as to why she paid you that much money? While further explaining the word 'PUSH' beside your name. Before you begin to talk about it. I have one question. And as the captain of the police department, I have to ask you if an investigator would ask. Did you push those boys into harm's way?"

"ABSOLUTELY NOT BRUCE!"

"You know me all too well Bruce Adams, I would never commit a crime like that, to anyone, for anyone, especially for money. Just what are you implying here?"

Bruce raises his right hand and points to the check ledger.

"Finish answering my question. Why did she write you a check for that much money?"

Broken Sanity

"Bruce you have it all wrong. You see Lucie felt so bad for those two boys. She asked me to split this money between the families to help with burial expenses. She also knew if it came from a State Trooper no one would question where it came from or who donated the money. I deposited the money into my account and wrote separate checks so they could not readily trace where it came from. I told each family it was brought to the station as an anonymous gift with instructions the money was to be transferred equally to the families. Since it was all over the news they accepted the money without question. End of story Bruce."

"END-OF-STORY!"

Bruce sat quietly absorbing the information. When Tommy spoke again.

"You actually thought you had something. Didn't you?"

"Yes I did, And you know me too well, I have to cover up everything."

"Now get off my porch and go back to work."

"Just what are you covering up Bruce?"

"Keep your mouth shut, Tommy."

Last Night

Margaret and Larry were wrapping up their last night together before his planned deployment. Leaving the Grand Hyatt, they decided to have dinner at Oyster Catchers and return to the room for one last night of being a married couple. Knowing Larry was scheduled to deploy the next day, Margaret wanted all she could get of her aviator before he left her.

Now seated at the restaurant Larry addressed the wait staff standing at their table and ordered a dozen oysters as an appetizer when Margaret playfully mentioned.

"Bomber, you should order more than a dozen oysters. I hear they make you more potent in bed and tonight will be a night to remember so you better store up for later."

"Margaret my love, How could another night be any different than the other two nights? You have worn me out already."

"Well now Bomber, are you saying you are too tired of me already? Is the honeymoon over with? You can always order a bowl of cheerios instead and that skimpy nighty I was saving for our last night together will have to wait in the closet until you return from your deployment."

Larry looks up at Margaret and then looks back to the smiling wait staff to change his order to two dozen oysters.

"I thought you would see it my way."

Broken Sanity

"You do have a convincing way with your words Margaret."

"I have a lot of ways to convince you Bomber. Since we are now married I will be the one wearing the pants in the family from now on."

"Is it not a man's job to wear the pants in a marriage, Margaret?"

"Of course you can wear the pants Bomber, but I like wearing your pants sometimes also?"

"There you go with those words of wisdom, Margaret. You have a way of making me hesitate for a moment. Why would you want to wear my pants? I like seeing you in female attire."

Margaret needed to change the subject quickly. Looking at herself in the bathroom mirror that morning it revealed she was farther along than she suspected she deliberated whether it was time to let the proverbial cat out of the bag. Leaning forward in her chair she reached out to hold Larry's hand. Looking him in the eyes her lips began forming the words necessary to form her words she was now poised to convey to the man she loved.

Larry returned the stare into her eyes as the oysters were being placed on the table between them.

"Oh! These look delicious." said Larry as he released Margarets hand while leaning back in his chair.

"These should do the trick for later on tonight. What were you about to say Margaret?"

"Nothing Bomber, it can wait, you need to enjoy those oysters while they are fresh."

Broken Sanity

"Indeed Margaret. You can convey your sweet thoughts to me later tonight."

"I just might do that, Bomber. I have so much I need to say to you."

"Like what, Margaret?"

"Bomber, let us not rush things, we are still getting to know one another. We all have a past, some baggage. It will all come out at some point in time."

Larry stopped to reflect on the meeting with her father in his study. He knew more about Margarets past than she realized. Her father did not hold anything back from Larry. He needed to know the truth about his daughter before he made the final decision to marry her.

Bruce made sure Larry was well informed of how Margaret could manipulate his wellbeing and how she could bring him to a breaking point of his sanity. It would be up to him to control his daughter in order for him to survive a long-term marriage.

His finale question to Larry was simple. 'Are you capable of handling her?' If his answer was no, then he should pack up and run now to save himself. Surprisingly Larry answered yes, he was strong enough to handle her. Larry convinced his new father-in-law he had undergone several seminars on psychological warfare in case he was ever shot down in enemy territory and his daughter could not be that bad.

"With that said Larry, you have my blessings."

Broken Sanity

Bruce placed his hand on Larrys shoulder and Jokingly replied.

"I have a strait jacket in the closet if you ever need one."

"I will keep that in mind for later."

Lary was now finishing eating his last Oyster. Looking up at Margaret sitting silently watching Larry consume all twenty-four of the slimy creatures before him.

"Margaret, you have not ordered anything to eat. Are you not hungry? Is there anything wrong?"

"Honestly, Bomber my stomach does not feel well at the moment, and I think I have been gaining weight. We have been going out to eat a lot since we have been together."

It was the best excuse she could produce to justify her bulge and being happy at the same time her man was being deployed tomorrow afternoon. Margaret was relying on him losing track of time when they first made love down by the river while he is deployed. Her thoughts were troubling, was it his child? She deliberated. Thinking it made sense to inform him a few months after he had left would make it more convincing if he ever questioned her.

"I am sorry you are not feeling well my love. I can settle our bill and take you back to the room for a nap before we engage with each other later on tonight. How does that sound to you?"

"Perfect Bomber, I just need a little rest, I do admit you have worn me out."

"It is the toughest material on the planet Margaret, I doubt I have put a dent in the thing."

"I see you are equally articulate with words, my darling. Let's get out of here so you can get to work trying."

"I will go pay our bill."

Margaret and Larry held hands with each other thru the lobby, riding the elevator, down the hallway to their room. Once inside Larry declares he is taking a quick shower to rinse off from the stifling Florida heat.

Making a quick rinse off, Larry walks out of the shower room into the sleeping area with nothing but a loose towel around his waist. Stopping bedside to find Margaret face down in a pillow fast asleep on the bed. Deciding he too needed the rest, dropped his towel to slowly climb onto the bed, and snuggled up next to the woman he would now call his wife. Wrapping his arm around her waist he placed his open palm on her stomach. Larry could tell she had a little extra to hold onto.

Hours passed them both with neither changing positions nor moving away from each other when Larry found himself aroused while holding his lover. Margaret woke from her slumber feeling her man behind her and turned towards him to accept his love.

"You make me so happy Bomber. I never want this to end."

Broken Sanity

"I will make sure it never ends for us Margaret. You are my wife now forever and ever."

"How long are you supposed to be deployed? I hope I do not have to wait extraordinarily long for your return."

"I should be back within six to eight months. I want to let you know something about this deployment."

"What? If this is bad, please do not tell me now. Not now."

"It is not a dreadful thing. Since we are now married. We are allowed housing on base. So, when I return we will be moving to Bozier City, Louisianna for the next three years of my service. How does that sound to you?"

"What a fantastic way to start our marriage and life together. Yes Bomber, having our own home together is acceptable to me. Especially far enough away from my parents, they cannot come over uninvited."

"You do know your parents are welcome to come stay with us anytime. I would hate them to think they were not welcome to visit."

"Personally, the way my father is married to his police investigation work, he probably never will, and I could care less if he ever does."

Larry kept his thoughts to himself for the moment. The words from her father were echoing in his head. The advice he received did not come from a gentleman passing words of wisdom to this young buck, but more of a stern warning to be proactive and take appropriate action.

All Larry wanted and needed in his life at the time was to start a new life with his wife by his side and get her as far away from Tommy as he could. Without ever being told, Larry knew the child Margaret was carrying belonged to Tommy.

The Sun was rising on the East coast of Florida bringing a new day with it as Margaret and Larry Rawlings packed up their belongings and processed out of the hotel. Loading their luggage into the Nova Margaret posed a question to her new husband Larry.

"Am I to assume I have to go back living with my parents until you return and move to Louisianna?"

"Yes, my love. I have to fill out paperwork and get the assignment to be stationed there. That will take some time to process thru the Air Force system. Once I have returned we will be set up for the rest of our time together. Please have patience with this process."

"I will do that for you Bomber. No one else but you. Let's go, take me home."

Larry knew it was the best place for his wife to be while he was deployed out of the country. Having Margaret close to her mother during her pregnancy was the best decision he could make for her. As soon as her mother discovered her daughter was pregnant, she may bring them closer than they are now. Larry was not too sure about her father's reaction to the attention he would be losing. Although the two of them had discussed the plan in confidence in his study.

Larry pulled the Nova into the driveway of Margarets home. Before he could fully stop or shut off the engine Margarets mother rushed out of the front door and down the steps to greet her daughter with a warm embrace.

Broken Sanity

"How are you honey? Come inside and tell me all about your honeymoon suite. Larry, grab Margarets bags and put them in her room I know you have to get back to the base to prepare for your deployment."

"Yes I do Mrs. Adams."

Larry did as he was instructed then walked out of the Adams home. Outside the front door Larry stopped, taking a moment on the porch to reflect on his next move. Hearing the distinctive sound of the rocking chair at the end of the porch. Larry turned to look to his right. Sitting by himself with coffee in hand was Bruce silently observing everything.

The two men make eye contact with each other. Bruce nods with acceptance as Larry presents a thumbs up in return, it was the man code for everything, is good in our world, then turns away to walk back down the steps to his car.

Turning the key to start the big engine to drive himself to MacDill Air Force Base to begin his deployment duties.

Larry checks himself thru the main entrance to MacDill AFB and drives to his barracks. His duffle bag was waiting for him next to the door. Now it was a matter of changing into his flight suit and getting a shuttle to the hanger.

All military salutes conveyed as Larry enters the briefing room to finalize the flight plan and an hour later he is walking up the removable stairs to take his position in the cockpit of the Strato Force bomber.

Broken Sanity

Preflight checks complete, Larry throttles the engines. Powering them to propel the massive flying machine out onto the runway for takeoff.

With Clearance from the tower. Larry radioed to his other four planes.

"Time to roll out boys Let's get this party in the air."

A large crowd of military and civilian workforce gathered outside the safe zone to watch the massive planes take off one by one. All waving to the pilots with some holding American flags.

Larry accepted the patriotic duty of leading them on their mission. Like the old pilots before him he used a clip to secure a picture of Margaret to the console alongside the many gauges he needed to keep an eye on while flying.

All bomber were now in the air in flying formation. Checks and more checkouts between each pilot via radio contact continued for a few hours before the auto pilots were turned on, allowing them to settle in for the long trip across land and water.

Larry performed his job well, but his mind was back in Florida, reliving his last few nights together with Margaret.

Three Rings

Michelle Stevens ended her day by changing into her pajamas. A single woman in her mother's house since her passing. Preparing a chef's salad, she entered her living room to turn on the television. Leaving the volume low enough to hear but not loud enough to interfere with her thoughts and investigating a little with the white pages open, searching for the names on her list.

Where do they live? She pondered. If these people are involved in her brother's death she needs to find the motive that triggered her mother's heart attack after learning of her brother's passing.

Following her finger as it slips down the page one line at a time looking at the many individuals with a last name of, Thompson. There he was Thompson, Steve. This might be him, then realizes there are several Steve Thompson's all with a different middle initial.

With pen in hand, she begins to write the addresses listed for all of them when the phone on the wall in the kitchen rings. Placing the pen on the paper and moving her salad aside, Michelle stands up as the second ring sound off.

Moving around the coffee table she heads for the kitchen as the third ring begins and cuts off before it finishes, signaling the caller hung up before it could complete its cycle.

Strange she thought. Why would someone hang up before she could answer? Michelle waits a few more minutes hoping the caller would redial her number. Several reasons come to mind as she waits beside the phone. Was it him? Did he get cold feet? Several minutes pass and her stomach was signaling she needed to eat her salad. Moving away from the phone and looking back at it a few times before she sat herself down on the sofa to begin eating and writing down addresses again.

The third address and number were now on her notepad as she consumed the salad in between each addressee. With five more to go Michelle takes a chance on a needed break to relieve herself in the restroom.

Thinking this would be the perfect time for her phone to ring. She was relieved she could finish and head back to the sofa. Grabbing her remote control to increase the volume to listen to a crime story on the news. The phone rang out startling her into dropping the remote control. As she retrieved it the second ring was in sequence.

Releasing it onto the sofa she headed for the kitchen to answer the phone as the third ring once again cut it self-short of a full ring. "Dang it." She fumed at herself for not being prepared for the call. He detective instincts are in high gear as she contemplates the callers reasoning for ending the call on the third ring both times now.

"Some people are weird." She mumbles to herself. Once again corporal Stevens stands vigilante by the walled device, waiting for the caller to dial her number one more time and this time she would be ready.

Repeating the same procedure of waiting and giving up. Michelle ever so slowly walks back into the living room and sits down. Then waits in silence deciding to do nothing but sit and wait for the phone to ring again.

Time is on her side.

Time is the essence of humanity.

Time yields answers.

Time is her advantage.

Broken Sanity

Time never stops.

Michelle gives up waiting. She is tired, it is late, she needs to sleep. Considering the caller had given up or he had finished playing their game with the phone calls, Michelle picks up her remote television controller to turn off the television. Remaining on the sofa a few more minutes in resting total silence before rising, She walks into the kitchen, facing the phone receiver and its cord dangling motionless in front of her.

Breaking the room's silence, to yell out.

"RING DAMMIT."

No ring, her superpowers could not make the thing sound off. Conceding her defeat, it was time to have her nightly glass of milk from the fridge and head to her comfortable bed. Retrieving a glass from the cabinet and opening the single door to her refrigerator, the milk bottle felt cold in her hand. A half glass now poured, and the container appropriately replaced it back in the door ledge, she lifted the glass to begin drinking.

Lips pressed to the glass as tilting it upward allowing the milk to cover her top lip and flow into her mouth and down her throat. The first ring fills the air. Startled she quickly lowers the glass. With her white mustache now present she turns her head towards the distinctive sound emanating from the phone.

The second ring is now in full volume throughout the kitchen as Michelle quickly sets the glass of milk on the counter to leap towards the phone and pull the receiver from its base. With a resounding "Hello" she answers before the third ring can begin.

Waiting for a response from the caller she is met with silence as the phone's connection goes dead. Holding the receiver in her hand, Michelle could not believe what had just transpired. Her mind hears her words without sound, "hung up, what a chicken he is." As if she is talking to the receiver, then slams it back into its resting spot with a furry.

Standing there with her arms crossed, her heart pounding, experiencing anger, the phone rings one more time. Grabbing the receiver, she answers with a stern tone for the caller.

"If this is your game Steve Thompson, I suggest you start talking because I know it is you calling."

But the voice she hears next is not Steve's. It is his sister Kim Thompson.

"Hello, Catrina McDaniels I assume."

In her haste to answer and with her undercover name used by the caller, Michelle needed a moment to get into character before replying to the female voice on the other end.

"Yes, this is her."

Silence is the game that can change everything you know about investigative procedures. Michelle needed her patience to listen in silence for anything she could hear in the background. But there was nothing to hear as her caller begins speaking with articulate perfection. This woman was definitely well educated choosing her words well enough to make her point clear to Michelle.

'Listen to me carefully Catrina. You met a man in the cafeteria today, did you not?"

"Yes, I did. What can you tell me about him?"

Another moment of silence falls on the receiver. Michelle can hear the evening shower of Florida rain beginning to fall on her roof. As she listens to the sound in the receiver she can hear the same rain coming down. Leading her to believe her caller was close by or at an outside pay phone booth.

"My name is Kim Thompson, I will say this once Catrina. That big guy who blocked you in the cafeteria today is my brother, and you must stay clear of him."

"Why do you say that? How did you get my number from him?'

"Go to bed Catrina, we will talk again soon and wipe the milk stash of your lips."

The receiver changes to the dial tone signaling the call had ended. Corporal Michele Stevens is left holding her phone looking frantically looking around her kitchen for evidence someone can see her, in her own kitchen.

Replacing the receiver, she heads for the kitchen window to peer out into the darkness, her mind now racing with questions. Who is out there? Where are they? How did she know about the milk on my lips?

Frantically she checks the doors and window locks at every entry point to her house, turning out every light including the night light in the bathroom and hallway. Then place her pillows against the headrest of her bed, leaning back against them.

Reaching for her service revolver previously placed on the nightstand next to her bed, she removes it from the holster. Now, sitting nervously for the sun to rise.

Dawn has arrived. Michelle slips quietly out of bed; her legs are stiff from sitting in the same position all night long. Moving slowly from the pain in her knees she walks about the house, opening the blinds at every window, checking to ensure they were still secure.

Heading to the front door she opens it to walk out on the porch. Still in her pajamas, with her service revolver, tightly gripped in her right hand, with her trigger finger at the ready position down the side of the pistol.

Looking up and down the street in front of her house, she notices a marked state trooper's vehicle parked a few doors down the street from her house. Staring at the patrol car, multiple questions rang out in her head.

"What is he doing here? I never called this into dispatch; I am supposed to be undercover. Is he guarding my home for some reason? Who sent him here?"

Corporal Stevens needed to know what the mission was when she decides to confront the officer in the patrol car. Still in her pajamas, walking barefoot, holding her revolver at her side she made her way to the patrol car.

Finding the officer asleep behind the wheel she used the barrel of her pistol to knock on the glass separating the two of them from each other.

The assigned officer opened his eyes when he heard the noise. Looking out at Michelle he pressed his finger on the electric button to roll down his driver's window to greet corporal Stevens with.

"Good morning corporal." Said the trooper greeting his stakeout.

"What are you doing here? And who are you? Why are you watching my home?" Asked Michelle.

The trooper was still waking up from a deep sleep. Without answering Micelle's questions directly, he looked her up and down, then replied.

"You should go back inside and put some clothes on, especially a bra, your headlights are on. And put that gun away before you scare the neighbors."

Corporal Stevens was now embarrassed. She did not know whether to cover her breasts first or hide the gun she was clutching in her hand. The seconds of time it took to contemplate her situation; the trooper's patrol car roared to life. Shifted into gear to drive away, leaving her standing alone on the sidewalk.

Enraged at the actions of the state trooper, Michelle stormed away with anger back to her house. Getting dressed in civilian clothes she headed into the station to report to captain Pedronia. Michelle could not control her excitement. She needed to report to her superior. Breaking department protocol of first filling a report to be submitted for review and then included in the captain's daily report file, then placed on his desk.

Instead, she bypassed set procedures and pranced herself straight into his office.

Hearing a knock on the door frame startled the captain into look up from his paperwork as corporal Michelle was entering and closing the door behind her.

Please come in and have a seat. What happened to to make you storm into my office like this without first clearing your presence with the front desk clerk? What is the matter corporal? By the way, have you showered today? You look like shiitake. Why are you not in uniform?"

"NO CAPTAIN, I HAVE NOT SHOWERED. LET ME TELL YOU WHAT HAPPENED TO ME LAST NIGHT!"

As the words spilled from Michelles lips. Captain Pedronia took as many notes as quickly as he could. Asking Corporal Stevens to repeat herself several times.

Once she had finished it was apparent to captain Pedronia, Michelle needed rest.

"Please go home and rest today. I will look into all of this and let you know what I find. Until then go home and for your sake. Take a shower and put on some decent clothes."

"Thanks captain I will do just that. Please let me know what you find out."

"Yes of course. Now get out of here."

Captain Pedroia waited several minutes after his guest had left before picking up the phone to call his predecessor.

"Bruce. You and I need to talk. In my office in thirty and find Tommy your trooper friend and bring him in here with you. You both have a lot to answer too.'

Exactly thirty minutes later the two men Pedronia asked to attend a meeting walked thru his door.

"Close the door and sit down." Shouted the captain.

The two men sat patiently as captain Pedronia starred at them for a minute before he started in on state trooper Tommy Neelsom. Pointing his finger directly at him he began.

"Explain to me sergeant Neelsom. What were you doing outside of my corporal's house last night?

Broken Sanity

Before he could answer captain Pedronia turned his finger to point at captain Adams to ask.

"Just, what involvement do you have in all of this ADAMS?"

The two men on the hot seat in Pedronia's office sat patiently quiet. Saying nothing, Silently sitting with both hands in their laps. Staring at the captain in front of them.

"I see how you two are going to play this game. We can sit here all day if that is what it will take to get one of you to start talking."

"Captain." Tommy began to speak. "I know it is difficult pill to swallow. But we are sworn to secrecy due to the ongoing investigation by the F.B.I. we cannot compromise our position or the cold cases, since they took over the operation. You do understand, do you not?"

"Well then that is all I need to know gentleman. You can leave now. Have a good day."

"Thank you for understanding captain."

"Before you leave. I do have one question captain Adams. How did you know about the milk on corporal Stevens lips?

"What milk captain?"

"I'm done with you two. GET OUT, NOW!"

The A.T.M. Video

"Good morning, Corporal Stevens, What are you doing back in here this morning?"

"You directed me to report directly to you and that is exactly what I am doing captain. I remember more about my encounter than I did yesterday. You need to hear the rest of my story."

"I did, but not like this. Please, take a breather. This is two days in a row. Let me get you some coffee. You look like you need some and then you can begin. I will be right back. Sit right there and calm yourself corporal Stevens."

"Yes captain. Coffee please, Black, and strong. I have been awake all night long."

Captain Pedronia left his office for the break room to pour a hot cup of coffee for corporal Stevens. He began walking back to his office slowly to stabilize the full cup. Opening his office door delicately with one hand and a push with his foot he saw corporal stevens fast asleep in the chair.

Clearing his throat loud enough to awaken his visitor, she reached up to accept the hot cup of coffee now presented to her.

"All right corporal. Take a couple of sips of coffee and begin. I will try to write down everything you say this morning. You can also write everything you have to say in a report later."

"Thank you captain. Let me start with;"

Broken Sanity

Captain Pedronia listened closely to corporal Steven describe her day from the time she arrived at the college to her ordeal that night. Detailing how the phone rang out only three times, each time the person called.

Captain Pedronia was especially intrigued as to how the caller knew she had been drinking milk. Then the State Trooper parked down the street from her house. When asked, Corporal Stevens gave a clear detailed description of the trooper sitting in his squad car and how he reacted to her presence when she woke him up.

"Are you telling me, you left your house in your pajamas with your revolver in hand, Nothing to identify yourself as an officer of the law? You could have been shot young lady."

"No, I mean yes, I did that, but when I saw the State car I figured he already knew who I was. I just wanted to confront him and find out why he was there in the first place. Someone sent him to my house captain. Someone is aware you put me under cover. So, please captain Pedronia, tell me to my face."

"DID YOU SEND A PATROL CAR TO MY HOUSE?"

"No, corporal, absolutely No, I did not."

"Then, who did?"

"These cold cases are getting interesting. Please think really hard. Is there anything you can think of that the trooper did out of standard protocol? I know you mentioned him joking about your headlights. Think creatively for a second. Is there anything else you can recall when he drove away?"

Broken Sanity

"Oh! YES! I remember seeing a camera in the back seat as he drove away from me. It had one of those long lenses on it."

"Ok that is how he was able to look into your kitchen window. The other two times the phone rang you were not in the kitchen, and they ended the calls. The third time is when you were getting a glass of milk. The lens captured that and somehow he relayed the information of the milk mustache on your upper lip to the caller."

"I am still shaking captain. I am new to these undercover operations. Please do not take me off the case. I made a commitment to find the person responsible for my brothers' death."

"That we will find out. I promise you. In the meantime. Are you up to looking at a video today? I have been informed that the bank transferred a copy of the ATM video to us yesterday. We have been saving it for you."

Corporal Steven jumped up from her seat, placing the coffee cup on captain Pedronia's desk and exclaimed in a loud voice.

"HELL YES, LETS GO TO THE VIDEO ROOM."

"I think you need some more sleep first corporal."

'That is not going to happen today captain. Not Today! Are you coming or not?"

Captain Pedronia stood up and proclaimed.

"I am right behind you. Lead the charge corporal."

Broken Sanity

Reaching the secured door, corporal Stevens enters the four-digit security code and waits for the sound of the lock releasing its stronghold on the latch, engaging the handle allowing corporal Stevens and himself entry to the dark video room.

Walking over to her viewing seat that is now occupied with a comrade. Before she could say or ask anything the young man picked up a VCR tape and handed it to her.

"I believe this is what you are here for Michelle."

"Yes, It is. Thank you."

Navigating herself around in the dark room to find the rack of VCR recorder / players, she inserted the tape in the one machine that would project the video onto the largest screen in the room, then walked back to her seat as the young man relinquished authority of it and the controls to the system, to her.

Settling herself into the office type chair she looked up at the screen in front of her and paused for a moment to inhale and exhale a breath of air. Her finger hovering over an illuminated green button with the word 'PLAY' embossed underneath it.

Captain Pedronia noticed the pause and with a comforting voice, spoke to Michelle.

"Take your time corporal, hit the play button when you are ready. We are all waiting on you. This is your baby."

Broken Sanity

Her index finger lowered ever so slowly as it reached the top of the green button. With a slight pressure the button plunged downward with the pressure of her finger. Feeling the momentary click as the button turned red, queuing the video player to begin the noise they make, as the screen illuminated with the video from the A.T.M.

Not knowing the exact moment in time of the incident, the tape was forwarded and reversed several times until. Captain Pedronia yelled out.

"There, stop the tape, that's her. Margaret with her boyfriend. It looks like he is getting money out of the A.T.M. That explains why there was money found in the street when the officers arrived."

Everyone in the room had eyes on the screen. Corporal Stevens had an ability to manipulate the video equipment unlike the others. She was masterful at cutting out sections, saving certain footage and zooming in on an object no one else could figure out how.

"What is happening corporal?" asked Captain Pedronia.

"It looks to me as if her boyfriend withdrew some cash and is counting it out in front of her. It is definitely her captain. That is her, I can zoom in if you want clarification?"

"Not necessary, I can see it is her from the streetlight."

Broken Sanity

Corporal Stevens narrates what she is seeing on the screen to everyone in the room.

"He has the money from the A.T.M now and is handing her some of the money. He is holding on to the rest of the money. They are now arguing about the rest of it. She keeps pointing towards the money in his hand. Wait, why did she look back away from him? What does he see? It appears; he is looking over her shoulder at something."

"Or someone." Said the captain.

Another video technician points out to her.

"LOOK! Do you see the shadow coming into frame? It is a big person."

"I can see the shadow, Wait, look, Margaret is walking away from her boyfriend. There he is coming into frame now. That is our guy captain. I bet it is the guy from the school cafeteria."

"STOP, Do not jump to conclusions, corporal."

"Yes, sir captain."

"Look captain, the two men are talking and now they are arguing. The boyfriend must know the guy who walked up to him. It is a shame this A.T.M. video does not have audio. Oh boy the boyfriend is pointing his fingers at the big guy and pointing down the street at what I assume is Margaret just out of the camera's lens angle."

"Is that what I think is happening corporal? Is the boyfriend sticking his finger into the big guy's chest?"

"It appears he is captain."

"That is going to provoke a response he is not going to like."

Just as captain Pedronia uttered his words. His prediction became known as the room exploded in a loud noise when everyone gasped at what they were witnessing on the video. The evidence is clearly an act of provocation. The larger man lifted his arms; with open hands he pushed the boyfriend backwards with enough force to lift him off the ground into a semitruck that could not stop in time to avoid the body thrown into its path.

Margaret calmly walked over to her friend laying in the street. Body torn and broken then looked back to his assailant, watching him turn and walk out of the camera's lens angle.

A knock at the security door reset the atmosphere in the room as captain Pedronia barked out orders to everyone.

"Shut down that video, No one is to speak of this, do you understand my order?

"Yes sir captain." said everyone in unison.

"Ok, now open the door."

Opening the security door let the hallway light enter quickly setting everyone's pupils to squint and guessing who the man was that entered the room. With the door now closed and secured it became apparent Bruce Adams had entered the video room in a surprise visit.

Broken Sanity

"Your assistant mentioned you might be in here Pedronia. Do you have any more video evidence to share with me?"

"No, we do not Adams. What are you doing here anyway?"

Captain Adams was looking around the room try-ing to adjust his eyes to see who was in attendance, when he met eye contact with corporal Stevens, then said.

"I thought I would stop by, since Lucie sent me out to get a few items from the store."

"I get it Adams, now how about you and I go back to my office."

As the two men were leaving corporal Stevens had a good look at captain Adams rear profile in the low light of the video room. Immediately she saw a parallel in the profile of his body and the large man in the A.T.M. video. It was him; she was sure of it. Although the two cold cases had similar end results, it was apparent the two cases had different assailants. The A.T.M. video was more at ground level giving a clearer picture of the assailants' back side profile.

The room had settled down with everyone now back on their assigned tasks. Michelle walked back to the rack of machines to retrieve the VCR tape for labeling and placing it in a secure safe. She played the tape again on her personnel monitor to capture a still image of the assailant in the video for saving on a disc later.

Without calling attention to herself she accessed the interior surveillance camera recordings of the video room. Selecting to view the footage on the monitor in front of her instead of the big screen that might raise unwanted questioning from her coworkers. The video starts out in real time. Selecting the play back feature. First selecting the appropriate camera to view, she scrolled to the exact timeline of captain Adams exiting the room.

Selecting, stop-frame-capture, Michelle Stevens now owned a still shot of captain Adams' backside to compare to the A.T.M. footage of the assailant. Nervously she retrieved a new floppy disc from a box on her desk, with one smooth motion, placed it in the slot on the front of the computer. The disc began to make the low whirling sound it always makes when inserting a floppy disc.

Looking around the room, it was apparent, no one cared to inquire into what she was doing. Looking back at the monitor's screen she directed the pointer with her mouse to shover over the save icon. With one click of her finger, she now had a copy of the images from each video.

With the low light of the room and her coworkers focused on their respective jobs, it was an easy task to remove the disc and place it in her purse. Convincing herself this is her evidence to help bring justice to her late brother.

She needed to get this copy to her uncle at the F.B.I. as soon as possible.

Walking back to Pedronia's office, Bruce stopped at the captain's doorway to excuse himself from entering and sitting down to chat. Mentioning Lucie was expecting him back home soon.

The two men shake hands and share a moment in the hallway. But captain Pedronia was too curious as to how and why his predecessor decided to come by the station on the day they were to view the video from the A.T.M.

How did he know? What did he know? Assuming corporal Stevens's verbal report of her incident and the description of the trooper. He figured the trooper was Bruce Adams' close friend Tommy.

Shaking hands to say good-bye to his visitor, captain Pedronia asked Bruce one final question.

"What are you picking up at the store for your wife?"

Bruce Adams finishes his handshake and pats the captain on his shoulder with the same hand, then turns away, leaving him standing in the hallway speechless. Within a few steps away from his friend he slows his pace to turn back towards captain Pedronia answering his question.

"Milk, If you know what I mean, CAPTAIN!"

Not Admissible

Corporal Michelle Stevens gathered her purse with the floppy skillfully placed in the bottom. Double checking herself in the low light to ensure she zippered it closed and shouldered it on her right side while using her elbow to keep it close to her body as if it were a part of her torso.

Standing up she bid goodbye to her companions, walked to the security door, and left without anyone suspecting she took home evidence.

Taking the elevator down to the garage level her anxiety had reached maximum level. Other officers were in the elevator getting off shift and chit chatting with each other as the elevator had been stopping at each floor for someone to exit and others enter.

Reaching the first floor of the building all of the officers and civilian contractors now exited the elevator. Reaching over to initiate the button to close the door, there was one more floor to go to reach the underground parking garage. Michelle was optimistic no one would enter before the doors could close.

"HOLD THE DOOR, PLEASE."

Michelle could see a dark skin lady's hand rush in to activate the doors' sensor, preventing it from closing.

"Well now, looka, here George. It is corporal Stevens. Wait a minute, yo in yo civi's. I see you still under cova. Ain't in no unifoam. Should I call you Catrina?"

Broken Sanity

Georga and Tina have a good laugh while the doors begin to close behind them. The elevator now descends to the garage as George speaks to corporal Stevens.

"We were heading over to your house to install a new wire today. Are you heading home?"

"Yes, I am, but I will not need the wire until later today. I have some unexpected business to attend to first. I can call into the station to let you know when I am ready. Will that be ok with you two jokers?"

If looks could harm a person. It was the look on Michelle's face that they needed to stray away from. Speechless, the two look at each other and nod their heads in unison. Both knew they had pushed Michelle's button, and it was time to leave her alone and back off.

The elevator slowed to a stop, with the doors wide open corporal Steven said nothing to her elevator companions, as she departed, leaving them standing inside. Without looking back, she held her head high and her purse clutched close to her body. It was now a brisk walk to her car.

Reaching her driveway, Michelle stopped her car and sat still in the car with the doors locked for a few moments before stepping out of the vehicle. She needed to convince herself; her surroundings were safe and secure before doing so.

Nothing was out of place, just a kid on a bicycle riding in her direction on the sidewalk. Her windows and door lock had not been broken or tampered with as she placed the key into the lock and with one swift motion she was inside, and the door slammed shut behind her. Now securing the lock on the handle and turning the dead bolt, she finally felt safe.

Heading to the kitchen phone to call her uncle and ask for a meeting with him at the F.B.I. field office.

Dialing the number and entering his extension she was hoping her uncle would answer. Instead of Roger answering, the call was auto transferred to another agent on duty.

"Hello, you have called the F.B.I. field office. Agent Davis here. How can I help you?"

"Agent Davis, this is Agent Thompson's sister Michelle. Where is my brother? I have to talk to him as soon as possible."

"Hi Michelle. Your brother is out for a couple of days. I am not supposed to tell you where he is, but since you are his sister I have no problem letting you know he is out on assignment. And the details of the assignment, I cannot divulge. Do you want me to leave him a note on his desk to call you when he gets back in the office?"

"Yes, please do that, and if you could do me a big favor. If he calls in at any time before that. Let him know, I have some especially valuable information for the two cold cases he is working on."

"That is what he is working on Michelle. Now I did not tell you that. So, it did not come from me, Ok?"

"Thank you agent Davis, I owe you one."

Michelle Stevens double checked every window and door lock once again before heading into her shower to clean herself before heading to bed. She was drastically tired from being awake all night and going into the station.

Broken Sanity

Finished and dried off. The fresh set of flannel pajamas comforted her with a warm feeling. Grabbing her nightly drink of milk from the refrigerator, she bypassed the glass and drank from the carton. Slowly she wipes the white mustache from her lips with a towel while her mind traveled back to the night before and the phone call referencing the white substance on her lips. The caller knew it was milk. Her mind wandered back in time to ponder.

"She saw everything. Getting the milk, watching me pour the milk, drink the milk, or was it really her that saw me drink the milk?"

Turning away from the refrigerator she glanced over at the phone on the wall one last time before she headed to her bedroom. Now horizontal and under her covers, she leaned over to the nightstand to check her revolver. Yes, it was loaded with a round in the chamber. She was ready to defend herself if it was necessary. Then she reached for the lamp cord to turn out the light.

It was early the next morning; Michelle was jolted out of bed when she realized the phone in the kitchen was ringing nonstop. Glancing at her alarm clock, it was five A.M. Think who would be so rude to call a person this early in the morning, she rushed into the kitchen to garb the receiver to stop the ringing that was hurting her ears. Immediately she begins to think it is her last caller, calling her again.

With a scratchy but stern morning voice she yells into the phone's receiver.

"HELLO!, who is this calling me this early? What do you want from me?"

Broken Sanity

"Calm down Michelle, this is your uncle Roger calling you. Agent Davis mentioned you called the bureau looking for me."

"Oh! Hello Uncle Roger. Yes I have a piece of evidence to show you that it may solve one of the cold cases. When can we get together?"

"I will be back in my office later today. Come in around five O'clock when most of the staff is gone for the day." Will that work for you? Drive around to the back and park in the rear parking lot. I will be at the rear entrance waiting to let you in."

"Perfect. See you then."

Arriving at the bureau, Michelle drove her car to the rear of the building as her uncle instructed and found an empty space near the rear door of the building. Leaving her vehicle, she followed her uncles' instructions to meet at the rear door. The camera overhead must have given him notification she had arrived when he opened it from the inside allowing her to enter the building.

Greeting her uncle with a family hug she stepped back to ask, "Where is your office? Better yet can we go to a video room? I have a floppy disc with still photos on it."

"We can use my office computer for that first. Then a larger screen if needed."

"Ok, I will follow you. Lead the way."

"I hope you are in shape. We will be using the back stairs to the fifth floor to avoid contact with other agents left hanging around."

"I do understand procedures and protocol, but this seems extreme to me, Uncle Roger."

Broken Sanity

"I will explain everything when we get to my office."

Walking the five flights of stairs was quick and easy. Agent Rogers pressed on the push bar to open the steel door into the hallway. A short distance away from the stairway, he turned to the right into a small interior walled office without a window.

"My office is right here near the exit. Come in and have a seat. My tenure here at the bureau is a short one so I do not have seniority. All I am allowed to use is this space for an office. It was a broom closet at one time."

Michelle giggles at her Uncles joke while seating herself in the cramped space.

"Not much legroom in here. Please make yourself comfortable as you can. Now down to business. What evidence have you brought me to look at?"

Michelle opens her purse to collect the floppy disc she diligently placed in a side zipper pocket. Retrieving it she held it up for display between two fingers.

"THIS." I have this."

"I see a floppy disc. What is on it? How did you acquire it? Do you have paperwork to transfer it to the F.B.I.? I will need to see that so I can log it in as evidence."

"What are you asking me? I have evidence on this. You have to look at it right away. I can do the paperwork later. Right now, you must look at what is on this disc. I can explain what you will be looking at."

"My niece are you indicating you do not have the proper paperwork to transfer that disc in your fingers and the evidence it has on it. To me or to the Bureau for that matter?

"NO! I did not know I needed paperwork or that it was necessary to show you evidence. If you look at the images I have on the disc you will come to the same conclusion as I have. You will see and know who pushed Margaret Adams boyfriend into a speeding truck."

"Michelle, you are a sworn officer of the law. You, above all others, should know you have to follow protocol in order to secure a concrete conviction in this case or any other cases in a court of law. When a fancy defense lawyer finds out you did not follow procedures, he will get this thrown out of court before anyone sees it. So, I have one question for you. How did you acquire this evidence?

"I took it from the video room when I was viewing the A.T.M. recordings the bank transferred to us. And when."

"STOP RIGHT THERE, I cannot believe I am hearing you say this. Michelle I cannot look at this or accept this evidence you have at this time. Did anyone see you take this disc from the video room?"

"No. I was very careful to not let anyone see what I was doing."

Broken Sanity

"Are you telling me, you took it upon yourself to steal evidence from your police department, The very department you work at. Without permission, authorization or filling out paperwork as described in police procedures. Am I correct?"

"Yes, But."

"No But's, you have not only violated protocol; you have broken the law and could get yourself terminated from the police force you joined to bring justice to your late brother. Do you not understand what you have done here?"

Michelle lowers her head in shame after receiving the verbal lecture from her uncle. Her head lowered in shame from her uncle's lashing.

"I suppose, I was overwhelmed with emotion at the time. I agree I did not think this thru. What should I do now? I can take this back and follow the proper channels to transfer it to the Bureau if that is what you suggest."

"I suggest you give that to me right now. I will have it destroyed."

"What? Why destroy evidence?

"You do not get it, do you? If you take this back and present it to your captain, he will begin asking a lot of questions you will not be prepared to answer. This will start an investigation into you and the department you are assigned to. The procedures and policies will be changed, and you will be relieved of duty or be reassigned to a lesser job in the basement mailroom."

"I am so sorry Uncle Roger. Please accept my apology. What do you want me to do with this disc?"

Broken Sanity

"Put that thing in the trash can beside my desk. Walk out of here the same way you came in. I will not be escorting you out. I have already risked my career talking to you about this. Let me make it clear. This meeting and conversation never happened. Now go home."

Michelle Stevens raised herself from her seated position, leaned over her Uncles desk and deposited the floppy in the wire basket he used for an office trash can. With an embarrassing wave of her hand to signal goodbye she left her Uncles' office and the Bureau down the back stairway and out the rear entrance.

Agent Roger Stevens waited at his desk long enough to ensure his niece had left the building. Leaned over his desk and retrieved the floppy setting it on his desk while he collected a new manilla folder from a file cabinet behind him. Opening the folder, he placed the disc in the middle and secured it with a piece of tape to prevent it from slipping out.

Using a bold pencil from his pencil holder he labeled the folder 'Michelle' and placed the file in the very back of the file cabinet next to the other two files marked 'cold cases.'

Corporal Michelle spends her night contemplating her schedule for the next day. When she awakens the next morning she made the call into the department to inform Tina and George that she was ready for another fitting. It was time to get back to her undercover duties.

Broken Sanity

Once fitted Michelle was ready to play the role of the undercover civilian, Catrina McDaniels. She was now off to the college to find the big man she was warned to stay away from. It was time to discover why she was told to do so.

Where to start looking was a no brainer as she headed straight for the cafeteria. Figuring he did not get that big by starving himself. Big boys are always eating.

Entering the large area filled with students sitting, eating, studying, and chatting with each other she spotted her target right away. There was no mistake, it was him. The biggest guy in the room was sitting with friends and wearing the same football jersey from her first encounter.

Focusing in on her target she weaved herself thru the gauntlet of tables and chairs as if she were a racehorse with blinders to prevent peripheral vision, she headed straight for the finish line when."

"Whoa! I did not see you standing there. Where did you come from?"

Michelle came to a complete stop. Standing in front of her was Kim. Her targets sister. The intense stand-off begins with an angry stare from a concerned sister. She intentionally blocked her path from continuing towards her brother, the same way he had blocked her days before.

Stepping closer to corporal Michelle, she leans into the microphone between her breasts to say.

"We know what you are doing here, and we know who you are. So, my suggestion is for you to turn your tail and leave this campus immediately, and do not return. You are not going to find what you are looking for in here anyway."

Michelle took the advice, deciding to leave the cafeteria and the campus. She drove home to remove the equipment microphone and recording device from her body. Thinking to herself.

"I am not cut out for this type of work."

Broken Sanity

Pool Side

The new Margaret Rawlings struggled to get out of bed as the nausea created a problem standing up. Her stomach was in knots. Heading to the toilet she heaved heavily into it. Even though she felt the need, nothing was coming out. Luckily, her parents were not home at the time to hear her morning ritual.

Out of the bedroom she could smell the coffee her mother left for her. Getting a fresh cup out of the cupboard she found a note taped to the door of the cabinet.

'I am out shopping for groceries, will be back shortly. Let's lay out by the pool today. We need to work on our tan lines.'

"Love you'

Mother

"Tan lines she thought, "Well it is about time she sees my baby bump. I wonder what she will say to me when she sees it?"

After finishing her coffee, Margaret returned to her room. Staring at her dresser, she hesitates to open the bottom drawer where her bathing suits were neatly stored. Bending down she opens the drawer to reveal the number of bathing suite styles she owned.

"I think today is going to be a one-piece day. No need to look fat in a two-piece. Mom is going to have questions when she sees me flopping around on the lounge chair like a beached seal."

Broken Sanity

Without hesitation Margaret selects a bright red one-piece suit to wear. Conversations with her mother kept her sanity to a minimum. Moms know the stress of dating and selecting a good man to marry and Larry was that man. It was a relief that her mom and father accepted Larry right away. Why they both liked him as much as she did will always be a question she would find the answer to someday, but for now she was a happy woman.

Slipping on the bathing suit she selected a large beach towel from the hall closet as a wrap to temporarily hide her stomach from her mother's inquisitive eyesight. Before stepping out of the glass doors to the pool side she poured herself a glass of sweet Southern tea. No wine today or until after the baby is born. She was sure mother would understand once she knew her reason for the abstinence.

Outside at the pool Margaret selected her favorite wooden Adirondack style chair as she settled in, leaning back to allowing the sun's rays to warm her body and the baby inside her as she waits for her mother to come home and join her pool side.

Margaret heard her mother's car enter the garage and close the California door sealing her inside. Stepping out she grabs the few bags of groceries to enter the house thru the garage door leading into the kitchen. Scurrying around taking little time to store the canned and refrigerated goods.

Looking out the sliding glass doors she notices her daughter is already outside soaking up the sun's rays. Lucynda peers out through the glass staring at her daughter basking in the sun. Her internal thoughts begin with how strikingly beautiful her daughter looked laying in the sun.

Broken Sanity

Her own youth flashed back to her of the days her body adorned the same young beauty. Oh! how her daddy worried for the boys she dated. He did not worry about her, just the boys that would need therapy after she had broken down their sanity.

She had a way of leading them astray. Bruce was the only man in her life that gave her the stability to marry him and not the others. Her moment was now finished. She needed to change into her bathing suit and join her daughter in the sun.

Margaret heard the glass door slide open. Lifting her sunglasses she could see her mother approaching.

"Hey mom" was all she said.

"Hey Margaret. Are you getting enough sun on you for a nice tan?"

"Yes, mother it is a nice warm day for this. How was the crowd at the supermarket? I bet you did not buy much. I know how you despise shopping with all those people around you."

"You know me well my daughter. I bought what I needed then got the hell out of there. Why are you covering your midsection with a beach towel? And why are you in a one-piece bathing suit? You always wear your stringy bikini's?"

Margaret removed the towel to reveal her midsection to her mother. It was time to let her mother know she was with a child.

Broken Sanity

"Oh! Margaret have you been gaining weight? I know you and Larry have been eating out a lot since you've been together. Take my advice, men want their women to stay slim for them. I have a diet plan that has worked thru the years for me. If you are interested in starting it?"

Margaret turned her head away from her mother, not saying a word to her as she thought.

'She will catch on soon enough.'

Lucynda continued to talk and rant about anything on her mind. Margaret love to sit out by the pool and listen to her mother's stories as she drank her wine. Margaret referred to it as the talking wine. It helped to intensify the stories her mother chose to convey. This day was no different as the wine helped her mother relax and give advice to her daughter about life and her new marriage to Larry.

On this day, her mother's words were falling on deaf ears. She had one thing that consumed her mind. The advice, her mother ramble about for hours had nothing to do with what she really needed to know. In the middle of the talking, lip flapping from her mother. Margaret turned her head to look at her through her sunglasses and abruptly interrupted her mother's train of thought, as she shouts out to stall the constant flow of words from her."

"MOTHER!" She shouted to gain her attention.

"What dear? I know, I am talking too much. I will shut up for a minute. Is there something you need to tell me honey?"

Broken Sanity

Margaret said nothing to her mom as she stood up from her seating position to reveal the bulge in her bathing suit. Facing her mother she said. Yes, mom there is something I need to say to you."

Lucynda looked up from her chair at her daughter to say.

"Ok, my dear, What is it?"

Placing both hands on her belly, Margaret revealed her status to her mom.

"I am pregnant mother."

Lucynda is caught off guard for a moment. Not sure how to respond, her mind wanders off in several directions as she tries to figure out the timeline it takes for a woman to show that much of a bulge before she begins her response to her daughter with the one question she could not answer herself.

"Well now! Look at you sweetie. How far along are you? Have you and Larry been busy in the bedroom or was that down by the river? Either way, honey I am happy for you. Have you told your father yet?"

"Mother, I would rather not tell daddy just yet."

"Why is that Margaret?"

"I have my reason I do not care to discuss right now."

"Well, honey he not blind and you are farther along than you think. How long have you been seeing Larry?"

"Mom this is difficult for me to say to you. But this is Larry's baby I am carrying. So do not go start questioning me."

"I had no intentions of upsetting you my daughter. You know we will welcome a grandchild into our family. I think you should tell your daddy as soon as possible. He may get his feelings hurt if you do not let him know. He might think you don't love him."

"I suppose you are right mother. Where is he anyway?"

"I sent him to the grocery store with a list of things to pick up. He should be back pretty quickly."

Lucynda had just finished with her words when Bruce pulled into the driveway as he looked up at his visor to push the button on the garage door opener. Now inside with the plastic bags of groceries, he looked out through the sliding glass doors to see the two beautiful women in his life having a mother daughter chat by the pool.

Stepping out of the kitchen to the sliding doors, he opened them to let the two know he would get his bathing suit on and join them poolside.

Margarets mother acknowledged her husband with a wave of her hand and a verbal.

"Ok babe."

Then she turned her attention back to Margaret to inform her of her thoughts.

"It is time to tell your father don't you agree?"

"I agree mother when he come out I will tell him. I can only hope he shows more enthusiasm than you did."

Lucynda could only muster a smirk at her daughter's words thrust at her. Then she picks up her glass of wine to take a large gulp and finish off the remaining wine in the glass. Standing up from her seated position Lucynda relies to her daughter.

"Well, thank you for that comment Margaret. I think I will get another glass of wine while you talk to your father. I think, you would rather I not attend the celebration with him."

Reaching the sliding glass doors, they automatically begin opening with Bruce coming out of the house ready for a swim. Seeing his wife, he leans into her for a quick kiss, only to hear a whispering voice in his ear.

"Your daughter has a surprise for you."

Bruce brushes off Lucynda's intoxicated demeanor as he continues out to the pool to plunge headfirst into the deep end. Surfacing he brushes his wet hair backwards over his bald spot and swims over to the steps to exit the cooling water. Walking over to a chair next to his daughter to proclaim.

"I sure need that dip. It is going to be a hot one today. What is on your mind today Margaret/ Are you missing your husband Larry already? By the way when is he scheduled to return?

"I am not real sure about the timeline daddy, although he did mention we would be getting relocation orders to Louisianna when he returns stateside."

"That sound good. I am sure he has everything planned out. If he doesn't he has plenty of time to figure it out. Is that what you need to tell me?"

"No daddy that is not everything I need to tell you. I was not planning to tell you this today, I did want it to be a more formal announcement, but I saw mother whisper to you as you came outside. So, I am sure she mentioned I have news for you."

"Yes, Margaret, you are correct. What can I help you with? Do you need some money? A new car?"

"No daddy, nothing like that'

"I am listening, what is it you want or need? I am here for you, whatever you need, I will make it happen."

Margaret looks at her father. Their eyes meet as Margaret removes her beach towel from her waist and stands up to reveal her baby bump. Bruce stares at his daughter with a surprise look on his face then Margaret declares to her father.

"What I need daddy is a stroller."

Bruce jumps up from his chair, knocking over the small table holding his beer. Reaches out to hug his daughter as tears begin to roll down his face. His embrace is stronger than usual, and Margaret reminds him to ease off a bit.

"Daddy, please lighten up. You don't know your own strength."

Margarets mother had stopped at the glass doors, to watch and wait for the right moment to join in on the celebration. Since everything looked joyous between her husband and daughter she decided to venture back out to the pool.

"It looks like you two are happy about the new member of the family coming."

Bruce was still hugging his daughter when Lucynda stepped up beside them. The only thing left for her to do was join in on a group hug as all three were now joyous with tears on their faces.

Bruce announces. "Alright everyone in the water, It is hot on this concrete."

Leading the pack Bruce is the first one to jump back in the pool as Lucynda sets her glass of wine down by the edge of the pool and follows suit into the water after Margaret.

With all three surfaced and treading water Bruce presents the same question to his daughter.

"How far along are you? How long have you been fooling around with Larry? Is this why you wanted to marry him?"

Broken Sanity

"DADDY, shouts Margaret. Please do not ask questions. Just be happy for me and Larry. And before you ask. This baby will not be named after either of you."

"Well, Lucy, I guess that settles that."

"I guess it does, Bruce."

"Ok, you two, I am going inside and shower. It is getting too hot for me and the baby to be out here. So, I will leave you two alone, to hash out your thoughts regarding my pregnancy and how you two plan to deal with it."

Margaret leaves the pool, dries herself off, then walks to the glass doors and disappears inside.

Lucy swims over to Bruce who is leaning against the wall in the shallow end of the pool and wraps her arms around her husband's neck, while holding herself aloft up-close to Bruces body as he realizes his wife had taken of the bottom half of her bathing suit.

Finished frolicking in the water the two headed to the chairs for some sun and conversation.

"I am really surprised Bruce this pregnancy happened so quickly with them."

"I am too Lucy, especially when Larry confided in me information that night they wanted to get married. You see, when him and I had that talk in my study."

"Oh? Did he tell you he planned to impregnate our daughter so quickly to start a family?"

Broken Sanity

"No. Lucy, he told me he was sterile, and not capable of siring children."

"WHAT? Then who's baby is she carrying?"

"Our daughter is carrying Tommy's child."

The Meeting

Captain Pedronia poured himself a cup of coffee from the break room and headed to his office with the nightshift report he had just picked up from the front desk clerk. Setting the coffee cup on his desk he positioned his office chair for sitting down for the first time that morning when again the disturbing knock rang out from his door.

His body tensed at the sound that announce someone needed something from him or a visitor had arrived at his office unannounced again. Ignoring the urge to look up to see who it is or to greet the visitor. Captain Pedronia reached over to lift the coffee cup to his lips, his head down looking thru his readers at the report file he had just opened up on his desk. When agent Roger Stevens from the F.B.I. walked in with his briefcase held in front of his waist with both hands, he clears his throat to get captain Pedronia's attention.

Captain Pedronia remained vigilant at looking at the nightshift case file on his desk. Head still down he says.

"From the sound of your voice agent Stevens. I assume you have come here to discuss something with me without obtaining a specific scheduled time to do so. I hope this is important enough to you, to interrupt my daily routine?"

Captain Pedronia finally looks up at agent Stevens to hear his reply with a stern eye contact.

Broken Sanity

"My presence here today warrants our unscheduled meeting. May I close the door, and I would suggest we sit at your conference table."

"Close the dam door. Let's get this over with. I have a lot on my plate today. So, the sooner you are finished and out of here the better off my day will be."

"Don't be so sure of yourself captain."

"What does that mean Stevens?"

Agent Stevens closes the office door then proceeds to the conference table where he takes a seat and opens his briefcase. Both men are now seated across from each other when agent Stevens begins to ask questions.

"How well do you know your predecessor captain Adams?

"I fail to see the reasoning for your question, but I will answer it anyway. I have known him for thirty years or more. I served under him as a beat police officer. For all of those years he has been a mentor to me. I would not have this job if it were not for his recommendation. Now explain your reason for asking a dumb question?"

"My reason for asking does not have to do with his police activities or his ability to govern this department. I want to know how well you know him outside of the department?"

"Other than the normal holiday gatherings here at the department. I have not had much of a friendly relationship with him. It is not like we were ever friends who were fishing or anything of that nature. Again, why are you asking me these questions?"

Broken Sanity

"The video's your department transferred to the bureau. I, um we have been analyzing the figures in them and comparing body size, weight, height, and the way they walk in and out of frame. The A.T.M. video has a clearer and closer image of our suspect versus the long-range camera from the bridge. All we have to go on is a rear image to dissect but I have someone in mind I need to discuss with you."

"From what I am assuming from this conversation. Are you are pointing a finger at captain Adams?"

"The Bureau has uncovered information about you friend the captain you may not know."

Rage is entering captain Pedronia's mind as he lashes out at agent Stevens regarding implicating his predecessor.

"If this is regarding captain Adams as a suspect. Let me remind you young man, He passed a lie detector test and so did his wife. I consider that sufficient enough to clear them both. Get to the point agent. Why are you here?"

Agent Stevens opens his briefcase to retrieve a piece of paper sliding it across the table to captain Pedronia.

"What is this?

"THAT sir! It is a stop report from a state trooper on the day your captain Adams participated in the lie detector test. It clearly shows he was driving impaired. Not drunk. He passed the breath alyizer clean. Did you know he took a prescription muscle relaxer to fool the test?"

Broken Sanity

"No, I had no idea he was even stopped."

"I am assured it was swept under the rug. He was the captain of this department at the time."

"I sure hope this isn't all you have to rely on agent. Because if it is you are barking up the wrong tree."

"I get your metaphor captain but let me move on from there. Here is an image from the A.T.M. video of our suspect. It is the only shot we have, and it is from the back-side of our perpetrator."

Once again agent Stevens produces a still photograph from his briefcase and slides it over to the captain for him to view.

"I have seen this many times. Please make a point and quit playing games."

"Take a close look at the figure in the photo and compare it to the figure in this second photo."

Agent Stevens slides a second still photograph across the table.

"See any resemblance in the figures in both photo's captain?"

"They look similar to me. Same height, same build, head cocked slightly to the right. Do you have a positive I.D. on who the person is in each photo?"

"Only one of the photo's is a person we both know."

'Who?"

A knock on the door delays agent Stevens' response. As captain Adams lets himself in. Leaving the door open. Captain Pedronia is holding the two photos in each hand still comparing them. Not understanding why captain Adams has come to the office he looks at agent Stevens while shrugging his shoulders.

"Good morning everyone, I hope I am on time? You two look like you've already started the meeting."

Before captain Adams can take his seat. Agent Stevens asks him.

"Hey captain, can you turn around and close the door for us before you sit down?"

Captain Pedronia has the two photographs in his finger as he watches his predecessor turn away to close the door. The hair raises on the back of his neck with a tingling sensation racing down his arms to his fingers. He has an AHA! Moment when he looks back at the one photograph.

Quickly looking over at agent Stevens with a shocking facial feature as agent Stevens grins at the captain. Captain Pedronia lays the two phots face down on the table as he watches captain Adams take a seat.

"Ok, you two. Why have you asked me to come in here today? Are we playing cards or talking shop?

Broken Sanity

"As I mention on the phone when I asked you to join us today. I have been assigned to the two cold cases regarding your daughter. So, let me begin by asking you a few questions captain Adams."

"I do not know what questions you could ask that this department has already asked. But, Sure, What do you want to know?"

"Where were you on the night your daughter's boyfriend was pushed violently into the oncoming semi?"

Captain Pedronia quickly forcibly intervenes before his friend can answer the question. Raising both hands in the air he replies sternly to the question agent Stevens presented.

"Wait just a minute. This man has already been through the ringer considering everything he had to go through and the thorough investigation this department conducted into his whereabouts on that night. Let me remind you of the facts agent Stevens he was clear of all wrongdoing. And furthermore, if you are interrogating my friend I will also remind you he has constitutional rights like everyone else. So, my question is, does he need a lawyer present before he answers your question?"

"Calm down captain. This is not a formal inquiring. I am merely trying to verify the same information you used to clear captain Adams. Now! If, I may continue without you interrupting."

"I can answer your question with a simple response. Everything in the record is my response to you. I am not going to repeat myself, nor will I add anything to a question I have already answered. It is in the files. Look up the answers to those questions yourself."

Broken Sanity

"Fair enough. I will refrain from asking any questions already presented. What I will ask are new questions.

How is your sone doing?"

Both captains ask the same questions to agent Stevens in unison.

"WHAT SON?"

"A man named, Tommy." Replied agent Stevens.

A long silence enters the room as both captains look at each other then look back at agent Stevens.

A moment of silence is what everyone needs when caught off guard. Captain Adams breaks the silence.

"I do not have a son."

"Yes you do." Replies agent Stevens.

"How is it possible you are so sure of yourself agent Stevens?"

"DNA, we ran your DNA on file, and it produced a perfect match to a state trooper. We tracked down his birth certificate that listed you as the father. Would you like to retract your last statement and change your answer?"

Broken Sanity

"That information and files were supposed to be sealed. It was a long time ago. I made a mistake. I was drunk at a Christmas party. My wife was not attending because she had the flu, and end of story. How were you able to get that information?'

"The F.B.I. can find out anything. You know that. Thus, the reason we are here discussing this and not publicly."

Another knock on the office door startles the two captains.

"WHO IS IT?' asks captain Pedronia in a loud voice.

The door opens to reveal state trooper Tommy Williams.

Quickly captain Adams turns to agent Stevens to declare.

"You better not say anything."

"Have a seat Tommy. The gang is all here. Said agent Stevens.

Captain Pedronia was now highly inquisitive of what agent Stevens had put together. It was now obvious that he asked the two men sitting across from him to come into his office today. But, Why?"

"Good Morning Trooper Williams. How are you today?

Broken Sanity

"Fine, thank you. Why did you ask me to come here?"

"I have a couple questions regarding the cold cases surrounding your friend Margaret. Can you give me your whereabouts on the night her boyfriend was pushed into a semi-truck?"

"That was a few years ago. I am not sure of where I was. Why do you ask?"

Once again, captain Pedronia intervenes before agent Stevens can reply.

"Tommy, you are not obligated to answer any questions without council present."

"I do not mind answering but I do not understand, Why am I being questioned here today? I had nothing to do with that incident."

"Oh, the bureau thinks you do."

"Please explain yourself Agent?'

"Stevens, agent Stevens. I am the special agent assigned to the cold cases."

"Oh yes, you are corporal Stevens Uncle aren't you?"

"Yes, Beside the point here. Can you answer my question?"

"Honestly I do not recall."

"Let me refresh your memory. The radio vector for your patrol car puts you one block away when the young man was pushed into the semi-truck. And to further give you cause for concern. The tracking vectors put you near the scene where my Nephew was pushed off the bridge that fateful night. Care to explain any of that to me?"

Before captain Pedronia started to speak to remind Tommy of his right to council. He raised his hand to stop him from commenting to say.

"I got this captain. I will answer you, agent Stevens with this official statement. That tad bit of information you just conveyed is circumstantial at best. As you are aware those state patrol cars are used by multiple officers assigned to patrol on any given day or night."

Agent Stevens never expected that answer. But Tommy was correct. He may have not been the driver of the patrol car those nights. If he were to pursue the matter further he would need to dig deeper into employee timeclock and dispatch information.

Captain Pedronia rises from his seat to declare.

"Are we done here? I think I have had enough fun for today. Goodbye Agent Stevens. Please come back when you are more prepared."

Retrieving the two photographs from the table. Agent Stevens placed them in his briefcase face down closing it while securing the two locks then slowly rose from his seat to bid goodbye to his company and left the room.

Broken Sanity

"What about the two of you?" Asked captain Pedronia.

"I'm out of here. Said captain Adams.

"Me also." Replied Tommy.

"Good, close the door behind you. I need to get back to work." Said, captain Pedronia.

Captain Bruce Adams quickly caught up to agent Stevens outside in the parking lot as he was reaching his assigned black S.U.V. from the bureau.

Both men stop to face each other as agent Stevens notices captain Bruce out of breath.

"What is the matter old man? Are you out of shape? Do you need a moment? You should sit with me in the car for a moment to catch your breath. Go around to the passenger side, I will unlock it for you."

Struggling to talk and the breath to find the words he needed to say, Bruce accepted the invitation and walked around to the passenger side to sit inside the agent's vehicle.

With both men seated. Agent Stevens starts the S.U.V. and turns down the air conditioning to cool his passenger. Getting a close look at Bruce Adams, he could see the aging man was now gaining control of his breathing and decides to start the conversation.

"Did I touch a nerve with something I said, back there in Pedronia's office?"

Broken Sanity

"You know dam well what you said about me having a son was wrong. Although, I have a son and his name
is Tommy. You played out a bold lie in front of captain
Pedronia. You know the Tommy who came to that meeting was not my son. I have not seen him since his birth.
His mother left the state, and I have not heard from her
since. Why did you do that?"

"Go ahead and lie to me captain Adams. Sit there
and tell me you have never in your career lied during a
briefing, investigation or played a card that was not true,
just to get a reaction or a testimony from a perpetrator?"

"Are you accusing me of a committing a crime
agent Stevens? Because if you are. You had better have
your ducks in a row and plenty of evidence to back this
up. The way I see it. You do not have any concrete evidence to present."

"You are correct captain; I do not have concrete
evidence to present a case to the attorney general at this
time. Although I am working on it. I also believe you have
covered your tracks well."

"No one believes it could have been you who
pushed those two boys to their death. You are a pillar of
the community and without hard evidence backing up my
charge against you, it will be dead in the water.

I do have one question remaining for you captain
Adams. If you did not do this. Why didn't your daughter
call 911? Especially when she saw her first boyfriend being pushed over the side of the bridge. The video clearly
shows her walking back to look over the side of the railing.
Did she know you would take care of everything for her?"

"I DID NOT PUSH ANYONE! Off a bridge or
into a semi. You are mistaken agent Roger Stevens. And
to answer your last question. I simply do not know why

she chose not to call 911. That video is just as disturbing to you as it is to me. Now leave me and my family alone."

"Sorry, no can do, now get out of my S.U.V. and get yourself to a doctor to find out why you cannot breathe."

Bruce turns away as he opens the passenger door to exit the vehicle while slamming the door shut in anger.

Walking back to his own truck he has to stop and catch his breath once again. His heart is racing, as he struggles to breathe.

He senses something is wrong.

Bruce arrives back home and struggles to enter the kitchen door from the garage. Lucynda is about to start dinner for the evening meal when she senses there is a problem with her husband.

"BRUCE, are you all right? What is wrong?"

"I think, it is time for me to see a doctor. I have been having some trouble breathing lately."

"I will make you an appointment first thing tomorrow morning."

"Awesome. Now what is for dinner?"

Turn of Events

Six months have passed since captain Larry Rawlings left for maneuvers to the Island of Guam in the Pacific ocean.

Margaret was walking around the house for exercise. The baby inside her was kicking more frequently and her doctor mentioned it was a sign she was nearing the end of her time carrying the little package inside of her.

The phone rings just as she is passing the end table at the living room sofa. Stopping and sitting on the sofa, she picks up the receiver.

"Hello, my darling Margaret. I am making a quick call to you to inform you my flight group is relocating back to MacDill. I want you to be ready as soon as I get there. My transfer papers have already been activated, and we are moving to Bozier City, Louisianna. How does that sound to you?"

"Absolutely wonderful Bomber. We will be ready to travel when you get here."

"We? Margaret you said we?"

"Silly man, I was waiting to tell you the surprise or better yet, show you when you got back home but I guess I will tell you now since I have let the cat out of the bag."

"Please tell me Margaret. What is my surprise?"

"Larry, you are going to be a daddy. Isn't that wonderful Bomber. We have a started a family together."

Larry Rawlings could not bear to tell his sweet wife the truth about his accident and the fact he was unable to have children. His thinking was clear to him. He needed to look the other way, say nothing, and run with it. It was as close as he would ever get to having his own child and the family atmosphere he desperately desired.

The fact that Margaret was having another man's baby was ok with him as long as she felt in her heart it was his, it would work for the both of them.

"Margaret, my love, this is the best news a man could ask for. I welcome our child into the world. You will be a great mother, and I will be the best father ever. I will be home this weekend and we will leave for Louisianna on Monday. They are giving me a week to report for duty. We have some catching up to do in that week."

"Oh! Larry I like it when you talk dirty to me on the phone."

"Calm down a little my love. Remember you are pregnant with our child."

"I know. The doctor said this child is almost ready to come out."

Larry and Margaret end their conversation. Margaret stands up and waddles into the kitchen to announce to her mother and father that Bomber is coming home and they are immediately heading out to live on base in Bozier City, Louisianna.

"Margaret, what great news for the two of you. Bruce did you hear that?

"Yes Lucy, I am sitting right here beside you."

Broken Sanity

Bruce refrained from showing as much emotion at the announcement. He always wanted his daughter to marry a man and get out of the house. But not while she is pregnant with another man's child. It did not work out as he envisioned, but he accepted the situation under the circumstances. At least a man was in her life that was willing to accept the responsibility of taking care of her.

His only hope was she did not break his sanity at some point in her life as she did with two other men in her life.

"Bruce, order a pizza for dinner. Your daughter and I have to start packing her stuff for the trip. Come on Margaret, let me get the extra luggage out of the attic. I will hand it down to you. I am so excited."

Bruce sits quietly in the chair at the kitchen table, listening to the two women in his life go on and on like cackling chickens in a henhouse. His lungs were burning. There is a lot for him to think about. Especially after today's encounter with agent Stevens. For that reason, his thoughts began to race around in his head. He hears words forming in his mind and contemplates.

{Here I am worrying about Larry's sanity, and It is my sanity I should be worried about. I need a beer and a cigarette right now.}

Broken Sanity

The next morning, he reminds his wife to secure a doctor's appointment with his general practitioner. Lucynda agrees he needs to get to the doctor and get some cough medicine after he kept her up all night coughing.

"You are scheduled to see the doctor at eleven this morning, they had a cancellation today, You are a lucky man our doctor likes checking me for breast cancer."

"Thanks for the extra information on how you secure the appointment Lucy."

"You know I am joking my dear."

"Yes I know, but I would not blame him. I like checking you myself."

"Latter when you return hot stuff. Right now, I am helping our daughter pack up. Let me know what he says when you get back."

"You will be the first to know, Lucy."

Bruce Adams is now finished with his doctor's appointment and decides to take a short drive to the beach. Indian Rocks beach is the place he took Lucynda to every weekend when they were dating and during the early years of their marriage before Margaret came along. It has been years since he walked along the water feeling the sand between his toes.

His mind is now still, holding back his emotions of days gone by and of the diagnosis his doctor suspected was wrong with him. Bruce deliberated with several questions of how and why his doctor was so sure of himself. Insisting on more tests. But the X-rays did not lie. He received reassured, insistence from his practitioner he had seen a lot of this type in all his years of practicing medicine. There was no need to prolong the truth with further testing. Oncology was out of the question. This silent killer was one tough sneaky S.O.B. He never suspected a thing until it is too late.

Bruce knew the answer to his diagnosis before the blood test and X-Rays were taken today. His time was now short. It was time to inform his wife. But how does a man tell someone he loves so deeply. A talk he never thought he would have to make.

It was a short retirement, lasting only a few years from the day he walked out of the department and the job he spent a lifetime working at. So, many things were planned and now it will never happen.

Bruce, he tall well-built man with a muscular physique is now standing at the water's edge, watching the sunset. Knowing his last sunset will come too soon for him.

His sanity is finally broken.

Bruce rolls his truck into the garage. It is dark and well after sunset when he arrives home. Composing himself he walks into the kitchen with the anticipation of Lucynda greeting him like she always does. Except she is not in the kitchen but in Margarets room chatting away the same way he had left the two earlier today.

Lucynda finally recognizes he had come home when he hears her yell out from Margarets room to inform him she bought Cuban sandwiches from Brocato's and his was in the fridge waiting for him.

Still coughing he passed on the sandwich and headed to their bedroom to take a shower and lie down. He wakes up abruptly as Lucy shakes him after several hours.

"Wake up sleepy dog, it is midnight. What is wrong with you? You never lie in bed when you come home. Did you go out with the boys?

"Um, Yea, I uh, met some of my old buddies and we had a few beers for old times' sake. How is our daughter? Did you get her packed up for her trip to Louisianna?

"Yes but we will need your help tomorrow to go rent a moving truck. She insists on taking her bedroom set with her. Can you help with dismantling it and loading it?"

"I will do my best and if I cannot call Tommy to come help?"

Lucynda slips under the covers and tries to get frisky with her husband.

"Not tonight Lucy, I have had a hard day, and I am worn out."

"Bruce Adams" Lucy shouts out loud. You never turn this down. What is wrong with you?"

"Tomorrow Lucy, please turn off the light. I need some rest."

Broken Sanity

Lucynda jumps out of bed. Standing over her man she insists he sit up and talk to her right now.

"Bruce Adams, what did that doctor say? I know you did not meet some of your friends because I cannot smell alcohol on your breath. Wait you came home awfully late. You did not eat your sandwich from Brocato's. Then you quickly took a shower. To top that off I know you went to the beach because there is sand in the bottom of the shower. Answer me Bruce Adams. Where have you been? You are not yourself and your behavior is completely out of character."

"Wow honey you should have been a detective. Although you are correct on all points. I assure you; I have not engaged in extracurricular activities to compromise our relationship."

"Then tell me what happened with you today."

"Let's go into the kitchen and make a pot of coffee. I have something I need to tell you."

Bruce sits patiently at the kitchen table waiting for his wife to make the coffee. Watching her dark hair with light gray streaks flow with her movement in the low light. Her Hair was her greatest asset. He used to joke with her, that if it weren't for her hair he would have married another woman. It was times like this, with her, he was so grateful they married each other.

"Here is your coffee Bruce. Our daughter is fast asleep. Now spill the beans.

Broken Sanity

Bruce started the conversation with all the information he had been gathering on the cold cases regarding their daughter he had assured himself and Lucy they would never get solved. Until now with the new evidence and how the new recruit's boyfriend had discovered a lost video of the bridge.

Taking a sip and coughing in between lecturing his wife with details she needed to know now. He described how the new recruit was the younger sister of Margarets first boyfriend that was first reported in the news as a bridge jumper and how the video tape showed a different story they now know he was violently pushed off the bridge.

Bruce further explained how he found out she was asked to go undercover to investigate her friends at the college as suspects and why he had asked Tommy to stake out her house to find out what she knew. The more information he shared with his wife the more interested she grew with what he was doing for the family.

He confessed to bribing the two officers in charge of taping the wire to corporal Stevens to say it had malfunctioned and to destroy any recordings the equipment had saved on its small thumb drive.

The part of his story that shocked her the most is when he had to tell his successor everything he knew about the investigation to convince him he was not involved in the crimes and merely doing some side investigation on his own. He was convincing enough after his talk with Luke Pedronia he was able to walk out of the department without being arrested and charged with tampering with the investigation or erroneously charged with the crimes himself.

"What, he actually thought you were involved in those boys' deaths?"

"Pour me another cup of coffee please. There is more."

"Oh My."

Bruce accepted his second cup of coffee and returned to the conversation. I had no choice but to ask our friend Tommy to be my eyes and ears. He actually had to threaten corporal Stevens's boyfriend so he would destroy the remainder of the video tapes he possessed, and face losing his job or serving jail time for not doing as he was directed to do by the city administrator. He uses some fancy law terminology, and the kid almost peed his pants.

Then he explains to his wife how he asked Tommy to lean on the bank and the branch manager to get the A.T.M. video before it got to the department. But Tommy was too late getting to him.

Entering the fact corporal Stevens has an uncle at the F.B.I. that she somehow convinced him he needed to get involved in the case when she was running her mouth about her new job and the video tape of the incident on the bridge her boyfriend gave her while they were at a family gathering.

'What is he doing with all the information?"

"This new agent begins asking questions and gathering evidence as he explains to Lucy this agent has now viewed the bridge tape and has questions for our daughter."

Broken Sanity

"What questions? I thought the questioning was finished."

"It was until the video showed our daughter walking over to the bridge railing to see if she could see her boyfriend floating in the water after he was pushed in."

"PUSHED IN? Everything pointed to him being a distraught lover and jumped in the water himself. You and I heard this on the news. This is getting weird Bruce. I do not know if I can handle any more of this information. Tonight."

"Hang in there with me, there is more."

'I am getting another cup of coffee. Do you want another cup."

"Yes, please."

Lucynda brings the final cups of coffee to the table. Handing her husband his cup the both lift their respective cups for another sip as Bruce begins another round of information when Lucy holds up her hand pausing her husband. They sit quietly for a moment. Bruce awaits her signal to begin again. Knowing she is absorbing the information he has conveyed so far.

It is one sip after another. Lucy stares off into the kitchen, refraining from making eye contact with her husband. Her head and neck bent low staring into the cup she has embraced for the past ten minutes with both hands.

Finally, it was time. She speaks slowly and softly. Not directly to her husband but into the cup.

"What else do they want to know from our daughter?"

Broken Sanity

"They want to know why she never called the police when she looked over the bridge railing and just left the scene?"

"Did she?"

"Yes, she did. The video is noticeably clear on that."

"Does it show who was with her?"

"Yes, Carl her boyfriend."

"Does it show how it happened?"

"You mean, who pushed that boy over the rail?"

"That is my question, Bruce."

"Yes it does. It also confirms two people involved. A driver and the actual perpetrator of the crime."

Lucynda turns her head to look directly at her husband in the dim kitchen light and asks one final question.

"Do they know who they are?'

"No, they do not. The video is not that clear. But I can tell you. They suspect I did it. You are safe, for the time being, Lucy."

"Anything else you want or need to tell me before I go back to bed?"

"The rest can wait for a later day, right now all I have to say is, I love you. Now let's go to bed."

Broken Sanity

"What about your doctor's visit today?"

"Nothing we need to discuss tonight, now go to bed."

"Yes captain."

Louisianna

Larry and Margaret said their last goodbyes to Margaret's parents. Hugs and kisses with gentleman's handshakes all complete. The local neighbors had gathered at the Adams household to help with the final loading into the moving van. It was now time to hitch up the car hauler supporting Larry's Chevy Nova to the vans trailer hitch.

Everything was now complete. With one last kiss from her mother and a final handshake shared with Larry and Bruce. They two newlyweds and unborn child were now on the road to Barksdale Air Force Base in Bozier City, Louisianna.

Lucynda turns to embrace her husband Bruce. Wrapping her arms around him as tight as she could without causing him to cough. She asks a sultry question he knew was coming as soon as the kids had left the area.

"Bruce my love."

"Yes Lucy."

"I think we should make up for last nights missed love. What do you think? The kids are gone now. I do not want to hear any excuses."

"I figure this was coming. Let's go inside."

Several days have passed since the house became an empty nest. Lucynda relentlessly called her daughter on a daily basis to check on her and the child that was due at any time. She repeated the same questions with every call she made.

"What are you having? Have the doctors informed you of the baby's sex yet? Have you and Larry chosen a name?"

Margaret responded to her mother with the same answers each time.

"No mother we want the gender to be a surprise to us, so, we told the doctor to keep that information from us. As for the names for each sex. Yes we have discussed some names, but the final name will be revealed when the baby is in our arms."

"Ok. That is the old school way of doing things. Please let me know when you go into labor."

"Yes mother, you will be the first person I call. Now I have to prepare dinner for my man. He will be off duty in an hour. Bye mother."

Lucynda's heart is filled with emotion. Her grandchild will be arriving soon. Elated she walks into the bedroom to update Bruce with the same information she received from Margaret. Her briefings were becoming annoying to Bruce. Knowing full well he needed to keep his feelings in check to avoid deterring her from bringing the daily report to him. She loves talking about the coming of her grandchild and maintaining her self-esteem meant a lot to him considering his diagnosis.

Broken Sanity

Bruce Adams. The former head of the homicide department and former chief of police was masterful at deception and secrecy tactics. It was his job to hold back pertinent information until it was necessary to reveal what he knew.

Hiding the doctors' diagnoses from his wife was different but definitely essential until their grandchild was brough into this world.

Bruce was holding himself as a pillar for Lucy. Although his plaster was crumbling faster than he wanted. Holding off telling his wife heavily weighed him. The two of them discussed the need to visit Louisianna as soon as the baby was born. Airline tickets would be finalized with a selected rental car that had been laced on standby for them.

Lucy answers the phone that had been ringing too many times. Her rush from the kitchen almost ended in disaster with a toe hitting the leg of the ottoman in front of Bruces lounge chair. Cursing the stubbed toe as she answers the phone.

It was agent Stevens on the line.

"Hello Lucynda. This is agent Stevens from the F.B.I. Is your husband home? I would like to speak with him."

"Yes he is Agent Stevens, but he has been sleeping a lot lately and he is not available at the moment. I will gladly let him know you called as soon as he wakes up."

Broken Sanity

"Thank you. I do hope he is ok. Did he get a chance to see a doctor for that cough and shortness of breath? He was really in bad shape the last time he and I sat in my S.U.V. discussing the case. I am sure your husband discussed details we know about the bridge incident involving your daughter. You know, the video showing a car pulling up behind your daughter's car and my distraught nephew leaning over the bridge railing. Well, there is no need to give further details. You know what happened next, don't you Lucynda."

Lucynda is stunned at the agent's accusation as she decides to respond before she lowers her arm to replace the receiver to its base.

"My suggestion to you agent Stevens is be careful which button you decide to push. You have no idea what this family is capable of. I will let my husband know you called for him. Thank you for calling agent Stevens."

A moment can seem like an eternity. Lucy is standing still staring at the phone now silent on the end table. Her toe begins to throb, reminding her of the sustained injury. Turning away she hobbles to go to the bedroom to seek a medical wrap for the toe she believes has just broken.

Entering her bedroom she stops to lean against the wall. There was Bruce lightly coughing and wheezing at the same time on the bed.

Forgetting her pain for another moment, she wonders. What is happening to her husband? Sleeping during the day is not normal protocol for him.

Broken Sanity

The pain returns alarming her immediately to seek attention to her toe. Her mind is talking to herself.

"As soon as I am finished with this toe I am waking that man up. We are having a needed talk."

The smell of food is filling the house. Bruce wakes up from sleeping all day and stumbles to the kitchen where he finds his wife cleaning up after herself.

"What are you cooking Lucy?"

"Meatloaf, with garlic mashed potatoes. Your favorite meal."

Bruce sits down at the kitchen table then informs Lucynda he is not hungry. The smell of the food is making him nauseous.

"Bruce Adams this has gone on long enough. What did that doctor say? And while you are talking, tell me why the F.B.I. called here today?"

"F.B.I.?"

"Yes, BRUCE THE F.B.I!"

"I told you last night you are safe. They suspect it was me. What did he say to you?"

"Not worth repeating right now. I am interested in what that doctor said to you. You have not been the same since you returned home later that day."

"Lucy my darling. Turn off the oven and sit with me."

Broken Sanity

Bruce begins his conversation with his wife. But before he could provide specific details the front doorbell rings out in the house signaling a visitor had arrived.

"Perfect timing Bruce. Did you ask someone to come over? Someone like Oh! I don't know, Tommy maybe?"

"Go answer the door Lucy. Please try to calm down for our guest."

Lucynda heads for the front door as quickly as she can with a broken toe. Throbbing in pain she slings the door open. Standing at the door with his trooper's hat removed is Tommy.

"Hello Lucy. May I come in? I need to talk with Bruce."

"Come in Tommy. You will find you friend in the kitchen."

Turning away from the door she attempts to lead Tommy to the kitchen when he asks.

"What happened to you?"

"Don't ask. Replies Lucy.

The two enter the kitchen to find Bruce having a coughing episode. Tommy takes a seat next to his mentor. Placing his hat on the kitchen table he becomes concerned for his friend's health. When Lucynda expresses her thoughts.

"Bruce, Tommy, I will leave you two here by yourselves to discuss whatever you need to discuss. Bruce will tell you the information he has yet to reveal to me about his doctor's visit while I am out of the room. I am going to the liquor store. I need a stiff drink tonight to relieve the pain in my toe."

Lucynda's car is out of the driveway when Tommy begins asking Bruce.

"What is she talking about?" What doctor's visit?"

"You are first. Why are you here?"

"I am getting information from my inside person at the D.A.'s office. The F.B.I. is considering indicting you on charges of withholding evidence in the two cases involving Margarets old boyfriends. They believe you are their main suspect but are having difficulty proving it beyond a shadow of doubt."

Bruce begins to cough uncontrollably. Tommy reaches for a wad of napkins on the table, handing them to his friend.

"Ok! Bruce, this coughing is not normal. What did your doctor tell you? When did you see him? And furthermore, why have you not told Lucy what is wrong with you?"

Broken Sanity

"Do you know how difficult it is to tell your wife you are dying of lung cancer? Especially when she is so excited about her grandchild coming."

"I, I, get that Bruce. I am sorry to hear this news. But before you say anything more about your condition. How is Margaret? How is the pregnancy proceeding? You know I am deeply concerned for her and the child on the way."

Bruce looks up at Tommy after wiping his mouth. He does his best to clear his throat to subtly say."

"Son, I know you are the father. So, do not play games with me. But to answer your question. And because you are the father with a need to know about the health of your child. Margaret and Larry are doing simply fine in Louisianna. They are happy the baby is on the way. Larry will take full responsibility of raising your child. What I need from you is a promise you will never visit that child in Louisianna or anywhere else they live. This secret goes to your grave. You never loved my daughter, and she never loved you. Larry and Margaret are truly in love with each other. This is my final request from you. Understood?"

"Yes captain. I understand."

"Good. Anything else you need from me?"

"Do you need me to create a diversion to get them off your tail?"

"No, Let them think what they think. You are not involved with this case, and they have no evidence to pin this on anyone else. So, let them work themselves into a frenzy trying to convict a dead man. You and I know the truth. This case will die with me. One last request before you leave Tommy."

"Yes sir anything."

"Go tell Pedronia."

"On my way sir. I hear your wife's car returning. I will let myself out. You have been the father I never had. Take care of yourself captain. Now tell Lucy what she needs to know."

Lucy walks in the kitchen door as Tommy exits the front door and places the bottle or rose' in the refrigerator. Turning the oven back on. She turns to her husband still sitting in the same seat. She notices the napkins resting on the table. They are soiled with spots of blood. There is no mistaking the reason for them being that way.

Lucynda breaks into uncontrollable crying as she rushes to Bruces side to embrace her husband.

"Why, Why have you not told me? Why Bruce Adams, Why?"

"You know why. I wanted to see you happy. Not like this. I am sorry Lucy. I do not think I can make the trip to Louisianna."

Bruce and Lucynda spent the rest of the night embracing each other and talking about the fun time together.

Broken Sanity

Nothing was ever said about the cases involving their daughter who now resides in Louisianna.

Closing in on the truth

Agent Stevens enters the police station with the intention of convincing captain Luke Pedronia to indict his former boss on charges of tampering with and withholding evidence in the murder of his nephew Carl Stevens.

Walking up to the assistant's desk to request a visit with captain Pedronia. Agent Stevens notices the current assistant is not the person he had been encountering on previous visits. This new officer takes a moment to assess the agent before speaking to him. He is a good-looking gentleman, with perfectly groomed hair, a pressed suit, and a tightly secured tie around his neck. She stands up from her seated position to look over at the front of her desk to view the man's shoes. When he asks.

"Miss, where is Tammy? And what are you looking at? If you do not mind me asking"

"Well, pretty boy, I do not get to see many men dressed like you coming in to see captain Pedronia. So, I thought, why not get a good look at you."

"Are you stalling me? Tammy does not do this."

"Yea, that's it. I stalled you. Go on in the captain is waiting for you. If you don't mind, I will be checking out your backside when you leave."

"Spare yourself from the view. That might hurt your eyes."

Agent Stevens enters captain Pedronia's office and seats himself at the conference table. While captain

Pedronia saunters over to meet him and sits on the other side to look at him face to face and begins the conversation.

"Let me get this straight Agent Stevens. You want to bring charges against this department's prior captain. A decorated member of the police force who has been credited with putting some of the worst criminals in this community behind bars for good.

Before we proceed with the discussion. Do you have sufficient evidence to get a grand jury to convict this man? Personally, you are on the wrong track, and this is a waste of this department's time. Tell me to my face why you feel you need to proceed with this formal accusation?"

Agent Stevens opens his briefcase to lay out his evidence. The still images the bureau pulled from the video tapes. Continuing with a show of size comparison of the figures in both cases were consistent with the same size and build as captain Adams.

More information was pulled from the briefcase to support reasoning captain Adams tampered with evidence in the case by grooming his daughter what to say to investigators.

"Just how are you going to prove he coached his daughter?"

"It is the Dunning-Kruger effect. The less the investigators know about what actually happened when Carl was pushed over that railing the dumber they would be to ask the correct questions, and no one is more confident that an ignorant person."

"Do you know what you are talking about, or do you just think you do agent? Are you defending this formal accusation with your arrogance?"

"I know what I am doing sir, and I will bring justice to bear on a man that is hiding the truth from us. His daughter is clearly on video looking over the bridge for Carl's body, then leaves the scene of the crime without notifying authorities of the incident. I have obtained a copy of her statement when she was interrogated. She swore to detectives he jumped off the bridge when she told him she was breaking up with him. Furthermore, you know her father was sitting right next to her when she was questioned."

"Let me interject here. Agent Stevens. That young lady was underage at the time. She requested her father be present during questioning."

"My question to you captain is this. Do you not believe he coached her on how to answer the question he had prepared ahead of time for the detectives under his command?"

"That is a bold statement agent Stevens. I take issue with the fact that you believe he would coerce his detectives to ask predetermined questions."

"You should look at this sworn statement from the officer under his command. The detective was forced into retirement a year before your predecessor retired. Pissed him off so badly he contacted us when he heard the bureau was getting involved."

"Nice try. I know who you are referring to without looking at the name on that statement. That officer has been written up on several occasions in the past for falsifying documents and making erroneous statements to ensure a conviction. I have a backlog of cases he was involved in that may require a new trial. So, a fancy lawyer will get his statement thrown out before the judge can read it. Keep it up 'STEVENS' the hole you are digging is getting deeper by the minute."

"Captain Pedronia I need you on board with this."

"Agent Stevens if you think for one minute, I am going to sign off on your wild goose chase. Then you do not know me very well. I was brought up to respect the law and trained by the best. One of those men training me is the man you are trying to convict with hearsay evidence.

I realize you are blood connected to one of the victims but that does not give you authority to falsely charge a man of a crime he may not have committed."

"All right captain, have it your way. I will continue to dig up the truth. I need to obtain the voice recordings from your undercover assignment. I will also ask my niece what she was able to find out at that college cafeteria."

"I have not seen the report or the voice recording, I have to admit to you. Somehow it is missing."

"You have got to be joking captain?"

"Do I look like a man who would joke about this type of thing agent Stevens? Your niece claims she followed procedures by turning it in. But we have no record of her doing so. It has vanished."

"I cannot believe what I am hearing from you. This is more reason to indict captain Adams. He obviously has an inside person working with him."

"I will say this again Agent Stevens. Unless you have concrete proof to back up your allegations, It is time for you to leave my office. Good day to you sir."

Broken Sanity

"I am not folding captain."

"Good, but until then, get out and do not come back unless you have substantial evidence."

The end of the day is near. Captain Luke Pedronia is now finishing up his daily routine and heads out to the parking lot to drive home. As he reaches his assigned unmarked car he slows his pace when he sees Bruce's friend and state trooper, Tommy Neelsom leaning on his vehicle. Cautiously he steps up to shake hands with the Trooper.

What do I owe to this remote "in the parking lot" visit from you? Did Adams send you here with a message for me to back off the investigation? Does he think he has the ability to intimidate me?"

"I think you need to hear what I have to say captain."

Tommy Neelsom begins to explain his reason for his visit and why he chose to inform the captain outside in private.

"Thank you for letting me know. I will keep this information quiet out of respect for our mutual friend. Although I do have one question I need to ask. It stems from a statement by agent Stevens the last time we met in my office.”

“What is your question captain?”

“Are you Bruce’s son?”

A small chuckle explodes from Tommy. As he answers.

“No sir, I am not his son. I can tell you he does have a son from a different mother other than Lucynda. You see he had a one-night fling with a woman just before he married Lucy. She did get pregnant with Bruce’s child and at his request she carried it full-term and delivered it. But left the child at the hospital. She was never seen again. So, Bruce found a suitable family to adopt the boy.”

“What is his name?

“Steve Thompson. Bruce always referred to him as ‘little Tommy boy,’ but he grew up not so little. Bruce dropped the ‘little title’ after he realized his child was now as big as he was.” He looks just like his dad especially from behind. He attends the same college as his daughter before she dropped out.”

“Does his wife know about this ill legitimate child?”

“Yes, she pays the bills for his college tuition and talks to him frequently.”

“Where can I find him?”

“You should ask your undercover agent that question. I think I have said enough already.”

"I know all about you and your surveillance of her house."

"Prepare yourself captain. Tommy boy is unstable. The surveillance of Michelle Stevens was a precaution to ensure she was safe. Especially after being confronted by him in the cafeteria. He spotted her as an officer of the law right away."

"I am not going to ask how you know all of this or why you are telling me now?"

"Two reasons sir. The man is dying. Lucynda asked me to tell you about the son. He has little time left, and the second reason is more important than the first."

"What could be so important to you?"

"Margaret is carrying my child. I do not want to see her go to jail."

Captain Pedronia stepped back away from Tommy as this information struck deep into him. He took a moment to digest the information.

"Well, Tommy that is interesting news. Let us end this conversation with that Trooper. I need to get home and digest all of this. I will call you in a couple days after I visit my old boss."

Captain Pedronia enters the Adams house and embraces Lucynda as she opens the front door. She begins to sob mercifully on her guest's shoulder. Lucynda releases him to wipe her tears away and mentions.

"Bruce is in the living room waiting on you. He is weak and frail. So be gentle on him."

"Thank you, lead the way."

Bruce is sitting up in his favorite chair wrapped in a throw to keep his body warm. Captain Pedronia immediately notices this once large man had lost half of his weight. Bruce attempts to reach out for a handshake to greet his friend and falls short of fully extending his arm. Captain Pedronia senses this and leans in to grasp the frail hand protruding from the cloth. A final greeting between friends.

Bruce's voice is lower than his normal boisterous volume as he mumbles hello to his friend. Seeing his friend in a deteriorated state is disturbing to Luke Pedronia. His eyes briefly tear up. Wiping away the salty moisture, he addresses the reason he had come to see his friend.

"Bruce I need to ask you some questions. I know this will be difficult, but I have to know the answers before it is too late, and I promise anything you say to me today will be held in strict confidence between us."

"What is it you need to know? You and that F.B.I. agent already think I committed those crimes."

"I admit I did, but now, I am not so convinced you are to blame, given new information I have acquired."

"I will tell you everything Luke. It is time to come clean with what I have suspected and kept to myself to protect my family during this ordeal."

Luke Pedronia presented the questions to his old friend one by one. Bruce did as he promised. No holding back as he detailed the entire episode of how Margarets boyfriends met their demise.

He told Luke how he met 'Tommy boys' mother and how he helped secure an adoption for the child after he was born when she abandoned the child. Continuing to talk in between coughing spells, he described how 'Tommy boy' was always in trouble with the law and how many times he had to cover up his tracks to keep him out of jail.

Lucynda joined in the conversation with additional information to corroborate Bruce's story of 'Tommy boys' violent anger and temperament, although he had a soft side for his half sister Margaret and always proclaimed he would do anything to protect her.

Bruce continued with how Tommy boy loved to play sports, but the college admins knew his test scores were too low for admission and football was the only reason he was accepted to college.

Captain Pedronia asked Bruce.

"What does all this have to do with the crimes."

Bruce looked over at his wife for reassurance from her to tell the captain what they had suspected all along. Lucy nodded her head at Bruce to signal it was ok to talk. Looking back at his friend he had tears in his eyes.

Broken Sanity

"Lucy and I always suspected 'Tommy boy' was the one who shoved those two boys into harm's way. But until I saw the video from the bridge. I was unsure if he was actually involved. It was the missing link I strived to find. Now we know he committed the crime by shoving them both to their death. I am sure it was 'Tommy boy.'

Although I will add, he does not understand the implications of what he did. His mental capacity to comprehending his actions is not there. In his mind he was protecting his sister from what he assessed was a potential danger to her."

"Are you telling me 'Tommy boy' followed her and her boyfriend to the bridge and downtown then stepped in for her self-defense?"

"Exactly."

"One more question Bruce before I go. What involvement does trooper Tommy Neelsom have in all of this?"

Again, Bruce looks at his wife for approval to answer. Lucynda nods her approval as she crosses her arms. Her lips are quivering while tears stream down her face. Bruce looks back at Luke one more time to reply.

"We believe, Tommy Neelsom was the driver of the car in the bridge video."

"I take that statement as circumstantial and not proven fact, correct?"

"Your assumption is correct captain."

"Thank you my friend. I will see my way out now. Take care of yourself."

The next week Agent Stevens and his niece were called into Luke Pedronia's office to discuss the information Bruce had passed on to him. Without revealing his source to them he spelled out his case against 'Tommy boy' and state trooper Tommy Neelsom.

A heated discussion ensued between the captain and Agent Stevens erupted with corporal Stevens adding her thoughts she was confident her uncle had strong feelings Bruce Adams was hiding something and he had to be setting up this 'Tommy boy' as the scapegoat.

Corporal Stevens was convincing captain Pedronia, Bruce Adams changed his story to protect himself and his family's involvement.

Captain Pedronia agreed with his corporal. The recent evidence acquired from his credible source needs to be followed up on immediately.

Agreeing with Luke Pedronia, agent Stevens discussed it with his niece who agreed he should ask state trooper Tommy Neelsom and Steve Thompson A.K.A. 'Tommy boy' to willingly come in for questioning. This would give them the comfortable impression they were not in trouble.

Broken Sanity

As the week rolled on the discussion of how to get the two men in the station for questioning without either knowing the other would also be there in separate rooms. This was the only way detectives could compare the stories in real time.

State trooper Tommy Neelsom was the easier of the two, a simple matter of scheduling him on his day off. His arrogance never allowed him to think he was suspected of being an accomplice to the crimes.

The challenge was to get 'Steve Thompson' to freely walk into the station for questioning. They dearly needed to get a confession out of him somehow. The first step was to find him.

Agent Stevens suggested the police department use corporal Stevens to venture back to the college cafeteria for a one on one with the big man. Several trips to the college proved Steve Thompson had stopped attending college classes after he heard his dad was sick with cancer.

His sister Kim was questioned several times regarding his whereabouts before she revealed to corporal Stevens he quit school when he heard the sad news about his father and considered his tuition would be dropped as soon as he died.

A dragnet was initiated statewide, then Nationwide to find their suspect, when the call come in from a Louisianna state official. They had a young man detained in the local holding cell matching the description of a Steve Thompson.

He was arrested as he attempted to gain access to Barksdale Air Force Base looking for a Margaret Rawlings.

Broken Sanity

Captain Pedronia provided details of the situation they faced with the two cold cases. It was crucial to have the discussion with the Louisianna officials to ensure extradition to bring the young man back to Florida for questioning.

"Why do you need him so quickly? What did this boy do?"

"We have to prove he murdered two boys. But until then he is an innocent until we can question him and prove he committed the crimes. At this point all we have is a corroborating story to work with. Now when can I expect delivery?"

"I have to tell you Pedronia, this kid was not an easy person to get in a patrol car. He managed to rough up a couple of my boys down here. And If you want my opinion. His cookies are not ready to come out of the oven."

"Thanks for the metaphor, just get him transported back here in a couple days if you can."

"Should be no more than two days. I will fill out the paperwork and get a couple volunteers to drive the van."

"Thank you for your cooperation. We will talk soon. By for now."

Broken Sanity

The transport van pulled into the holding area where all prisoners are taken out of patrol cars before entering the police station for booking. Once they were stopped inside the secured area. Two large gates closed in the van from the front and the rear. If a prisoner tried to run once they were outside of the transport. There was no escaping.

The two Louisianna security contractors stepped out of the van to greet their Florida counterparts. When one of the guards noticed a large bulge in the side of the van carrying Steve Thompson.

"Hey, what's with the bulge in the side of the van? Who is in there?"

"That my friend is from a size fourteen shoe hitting the inside of the van. You see we had six men attempt to get him out of the holding cell and bring him hear. He would not budge when we told him where he was going.

Only when one of the female officers mentioned we were taking him to see his sister Margaret did he calm down. I mean calmed way down. He pleasantly walked with us to the van and sat quietly. Well, that worked until he figured out we were on the road longer than it should have taken to get to the Air Base. That's is when he went psycho. That dent is from him kicking the wall of the van trying to escape."

"So, we should tell him his sister is inside to get him to cooperate and come inside?"

"You catch on quick. That is our suggestion, it worked for us."

Case Closed

The four guards are standing at the rear of the transport van deciding their next course of action before opening the doors and releasing the raging bull trapped inside.

Two small windows with wire mesh were imbedded in each of the doors when a face appeared in one of them.

"Geeze he looks just like our old captain Bruce Adams." Said one of them.

The voice inside attached to the face yells out of the wire mesh.

"I am not coming out of this van. Where is my sister? I want to see my sister, NOW!

"You see. All he wants is his sister." Said the driver.

"Ok let's try it this. Your sister is inside waiting for you. If you want to see her you have to calmly walk out of the van and follow us. Will you cooperate with us if we take you too her?" Asked the Florida guard.

From inside the van a soft manly voice replied.

"Yes."

Broken Sanity

The command came from the Florida officers.

"Open the doors."

"It is your rodeo now. He is all yours." Said the driver.

Calmly Steve Thompson stepped out of the van. Without hesitation he asks.

"Where is my sister?"

The two Florida officer were amazed at the size of the man they were now face to face with. The remarkable resemblance to their old boss became clear, no one could question this was his son. Bringing them back to reality he asks again.

"Where is my sister? You said you were taking me to her."

Quickly thinking the one officer replied.

"Follow me."

Leading their suspect through the halls of the police station proved challenging. All of the officers stopped to stare at the man who starkly resembled their old boss.

Walking into the small room with a steel table Steve Thompson was instructed to sit quietly while his sister was informed of his arrival.

The two officers walked out of the room after securing the suspect's wrists to the desk with handcuffs. They met captain Pedroza and F.B.I agent Stevens in the hallway.

Broken Sanity

"He is all yours. We are heading back to our area. Let us know when we need to come back to get him."

"I will go in first Agent Stevens, I know what to ask him. You watch thru the one-way glass."

Entering the room to begin questioning captain Pedronia himself is taken back by the resemblance to the man he replaced at the station.

"Good day. I am speaking to Steve Thompson am I correct?

"Yes that is me. I was told my sister Margaret was here. I want to see her."

"She is in another room talking to our detectives at the moment."

"I need to ask a few questions before I bring her in here. Is that ok with you?"

"Yes"

"Ok, let me start with this. Can you tell me what you know about her boyfriends that passed away?"

"I know she had problems with both of them. Now when do I get to see my sister? I have to make sure she is safe."

"Why? Did you feel she was is in danger?"

"She has to be protected from those boys."

"Who told you to protect her?"

In another room adjacent to the center viewing room agent Stevens could see through the thick one-way glass revealing trooper Tommy Neelsom being questioned and in the other room he could see Steve Thompson being questioned by captain Pedronia. Switching the sound back and forth from one room to the other he listened to the answers given by each man.

Agent Steven was clearly agitated that the detectives were too kind to trooper Neelsom by joking with him on matters not related to the investigation. But it was their tactics to get him comfortable before they began with the hardened questions about to be presented.

Listening he finally heard one of the detectives ask.

"Hey Tommy. Why do you think Margarets first boyfriend jumped off the bridge?" I hear you have been doing Bruces daughter, so we all want to know is she a difficult woman to handle?"

Trooper Tommy was so comfortable talking shop with his fellow officers her answered the question before thinking. In his mind it was just a couple guys talking about women, forgetting he was being interrogated.

"Difficult, is a kind description of that woman. Anyone dating her would jump off that bridge to get away from her. Except they did not jump. He was pushed over the railing."

The two detectives in the room looked at each other. Tommy had just provided the key information they knew happened from the video that had not been shared publicly and only captain Bruce Adams and the current department staff knew the boy was pushed from the bridge. With this admission they proceeded to ask.

Broken Sanity

"Pushed? You said "Pushed? We were under the impression he jumped. It has been reported in the news that he jumped. How do you know he was pushed?"

State trooper Tommy Neelsom was trapped and he knew it. These guys were good at getting a person to provide details no one would know unless the person being questioned was involved in the crime and he just provided the information they needed to prove that.

"Cat got your tongue trooper. You just went radio silent on us."

"I think I have said enough to you two this morning. Unless you plan to arrest me, I will be on my way gentleman."

"One couple more questions Tommy. How did you know where to find Margaret that night? Were you the driver of the car that pulled up behind Margarets car at the bridge? Did 'Tommy boy' jump out of your personal vehicle and push that boy off the bridge?"

"You got me once; I am not falling for this again. I know my rights. All you have is circumstantial evidence. So quit fishing."

"Sit here while we go talk to someone."

"Who? Who is on the other side of that glass?

The two detectives walk out of the room and into the center room to discuss the next step with agent Stevens.

Broken Sanity

"We have him where we want him. He knows the detail of that boy getting pushed instead of being a jumper. What would you like us to ask him next?"

"Unfortunately, the answer he gave to that small detail can be easily confirmed by sources providing him that knowledge. I am sure his lifelong friend may have inadvertently slipped up and mentioned it while conversing on his porch one day. From what I have heard they had a little porch society meeting quite regularly."

"You are right agent Stevens; we are back to square one."

"Notably it was a great try. Now go keep him company and let's see what his friend has to say in that room. I am assured he will clam up the rest of the day."

Turning his attention to watching captain Pedronia through the other window. He flipped the switch to listen in. Captain Pedronia was more skillful in his approach to questioning a perpetrator. Agent Stevens listened carefully at the questioning.

"I will get your sister when you tell me what we need to know then you and her will be free to go."

"What do you want to know?"

"Who told you to protect your sister the way you did?"

"It is how I was raised. I was bigger than her. It was my job as a brother to never let anyone harm her. If they did I was instructed to take care of them."

"How Steve, by pushing them off a bridge or into oncoming traffic?"

Broken Sanity

"I had to protect her. That is what I was told to do."

Captain Pedronia grew agitated and raised the octave in his voice when he asked.

"By whom Steve. Who told you to protect her this way?"

In an extremely low tone voice Steve Thompson replied.

"Lucynda."

"What did you say?"

"I said Lucynda. She always instructed me to keep Margaret safe. I was supposed to push him around and scare him into not hurting Margaret. I rushed over to push him around but when I did. I guess, I pushed too hard. He went over the side. I got scared and ran back to the car and jumped in. I was told he was ok."

"You were told he was ok? Who told you that, was it the person driving Steve? Who drove you to both of those locations? Two boys lost their lives because of you."

"Yes' I think, I cannot remember everything. I do not know what happened to them after we left. I am not that smart. My memory is not as good as a lot of people. I play football really well. Am I going to see my sister. I want to see Margaret."

Just then captain Pedronia realized the man in front of him had the mind of a child. How are we going to prosecute him for these crimes? He cannot remember what he did or who drove the car.

"Steve listen to me, I am going out of the room for a minute. I will be right back."

"Ok. Are you bringing Margaret back with you? I want to see my sister."

Captain Pedronia walked out of the interrogation room and into the center viewing room to have a conversation with agent Stevens.

"Did you hear what he said?"

"Yes, I did."

"Agent Stevens. We are unable to prosecute that man in there given his mental capacity to stand trial. We will be wasting time and resources. He needs help in ways jail will not be able to provide for him even if we are successful in convicting him."

A knock rings out on the door from the outside. Opening the door the two men are shocked to see Kim Steve's sister.

"What can we do for you the ask in unison."

'I am here to get my brother."

"How did you know we had him?"

"Unfortunately, I also bring sad news."

Broken Sanity

"What information do you have?" Asked agent Stevens.

"Captain Bruce Adams has passed away an hour ago. His wife Lucynda asked me to bring you this note. It is for your agent Stevens. It is from Lucynda his wife."

Agent stevens opens the envelope, Reads the words written on the paper presented to him. He then folds it slowly and places it in his coat pocket. Looks up at captain Pedronia and Kim Thompson to say.

"Take your brother home. I know you will do what is right for him. To you captain Pedroia. Go tell trooper Tommy Neelsom he is free to go.

Inquisitively Luke Pedronia asked what is written in the note.

Agent Stevens responds with.

"Margaret has had her child a seven-pound ten-ounce baby boy. They named him Leonard Bruce Rawlings. He was born the very minute Bruce passed away.

This Case is Closed.

254

I would like to give the most thanks to my sister Rebecca Allen Bruce. You have always believed in me sister. Without your strength I would never have succeeded.

To all the friends I have lost in my 69 years of living.

I loved you all like family.

Michael Perry Allen

I am a man that cherishes the outdoors. As I get older and gain wisdom from life's experiences. I now know the meaning of it. It is within all of us to hold ourselves to a higher standard and to pass on the knowledge we have learned to the younger generation that follows.

Previous novels:

<u>50 Million Reasons.</u>

A fictional story embedded in my head for years.

<u>The Evil Within Them.</u>

The true incidents of my life encounters after a divorce and the narcissistic people I had the displeasure of meeting.